ATTACK OF APOLLYON

Attack
of Apollyon

LEFT BEHIND®

> THE KIDS <

Jerry B. Jenkins

Tim LaHaye

WITH CHRIS FABRY

TYNDALE KiDS

TYNDALE HOUSE PUBLISHERS, INC.
WHEATON, ILLINOIS

Visit Tyndale's exciting Web site at www.tyndale.com

Discover the latest Left Behind news at www.leftbehind.com

Published in association with the literary agency of Alive Communications, Inc., 7680 Goddard Street, Suite 200, Colorado Springs, CO 80920.

Edited by Curtis H. C. Lundgren

ISBN 0-8423-4313-X

Printed in the United States of America

08   07   06   05   04   03   02

9   8   7   6   5   4   3   2   1

To Josiah Borg

TABLE OF CONTENTS

What's Gone On Before

Judd Thompson Jr. and the rest of the Young Tribulation Force are involved in the adventure of a lifetime. The global vanishings have left them alone, and now, with the Meeting of the Witnesses complete, they face new dangers.

Judd and Lionel Washington are in Jerusalem with their friend Mitchell Stein. When Mr. Stein is arrested by the Global Community, they stumble onto Samuel Goldberg, a boy who witnessed the deaths of Tsion Ben-Judah's family. Samuel wants to help Judd and Lionel, but his father works for the Global Community.

After a frightening escape from Samuel's house, Judd and Lionel meet another believer, named Jamal. He and his family give Judd and Lionel a place to stay. While there, they learn of Mr. Stein's miraculous release from jail. Mr. Stein then leaves for an extended time of training.

While Vicki and the others at the secret school search for former Morale Monitor Melinda Bentley, Mark rescues Melinda from certain death at the hands of the Global Community. On their way back to the hide-out Mark and Melinda find Janie, a girl Vicki knew from her days in the detention center.

Vicki welcomes Melinda and Janie but knows rough times are ahead if the girls remain closed to the truth. Conrad Graham discovers a safe in the bell tower of the old school but can't open it.

The next judgment from God darkens the sun, moon, and stars. The kids at the school huddle together to keep warm. Melinda asks Vicki, "Are we going to die?"

In Israel, Judd and Nada, Jamal's daughter, race to Samuel's house to see if he is okay. Nada is dragged inside.

Join the Young Trib Force as they struggle to survive the freezing temperatures and prepare for one of the Bible's most frightening predictions.

ONE

The Rescue

JUDD's first instinct was to jump from the car and run to the Goldberg house, but Nada had been pulled inside so quickly that he had no chance to rescue her. He ran his hand through his hair. The gas gauge read almost empty.

Judd left the car running and raced toward Samuel's house. Icy wind whipped at his face. He had lived in Chicago all his life, but Judd had never felt such biting cold. He peeked in the window, but the drapes were closed.

Judd circled the house. He found the secret entrance he and Lionel had used to escape through a few weeks earlier, but it was nailed shut. He kept moving, rubbing his arms to stay warm. At the back of the house Judd climbed onto the wooden porch and stood

1

on a railing to reach the bare kitchen window. He took a minute to rub a small spot in the ice so he could look inside.

Shadows in the living room, beyond the kitchen. Someone yelled. If Mr. Goldberg had pulled Nada inside, they were in deep trouble.

Judd was surprised to find the window unlocked. Carefully he pushed it open.

"You are with them, aren't you, young lady?" a man yelled. Judd recognized the voice. It was Mr. Goldberg.

"I was worried about your son," Nada said. "Now that I know he is all right, I will go."

"Sit down!" the man screamed. "You're not going anywhere."

Judd pulled himself inside, careful not to make noise.

He closed the window quietly and walked toward the living room. Mr. Goldberg shoved Nada into a chair. "How do you know my son?"

Nada looked away.

The man raised a hand. Samuel shouted, "Stop!" making his father turn. "Don't hurt her," Samuel said, stepping between them. "I was supposed to call her house to say I was all right. You wouldn't let me outside."

"What are you saying? Why would you have to go outside—"

"I've been trying to tell you for days," Samuel interrupted. "I helped Judd and the other boy escape. They showed me the truth about God."

Mr. Goldberg stepped back. "Traitor," he muttered.

"I couldn't call them from here or you'd trace it," Samuel said. "What they've said about Jesus is true. He is the Messiah. I've wanted to tell you so badly—"

"Enough," his father said.

"I have the mark of the believer now—"

"Be quiet!" Mr. Goldberg slammed his fist into a lamp and knocked it to the floor. "You're the same as Ben-Judah."

"Listen to me," Samuel pleaded. "Rabbi Ben-Judah is right. This weather phenomenon was predicted in the Bible thousands of years ago. At least let me explain it."

"The only thing I want from you is the location of the hiding place of those two."

Samuel shook his head. "I cannot betray my friends."

Mr. Goldberg turned to Nada. "Unless . . ." He leaned close.

"Father, no!"

"Perhaps *you* know where they are."

Nada glanced past the man into the shadows. Judd put a finger to his lips.

Mr. Goldberg picked up a telephone. "We'll see how quiet you will stay when we have you at headquarters."

Lionel Washington worried about Judd and Nada. Nada's father, Jamal, had watched Nicolae Carpathia's news conference intently. Now he paced the floor, asking questions. Each time Jamal asked about Nada and Judd, Lionel changed the subject.

"Do you think Carpathia means what he said about people who agree with Dr. Ben-Judah?" Lionel said.

"Carpathia will do whatever it takes to stop these plagues," Jamal said, "just like Pharaoh in the Old Testament."

"But if this is true, we can go home," Lionel said. "And Judd and Nada—"

"What?" Jamal said.

Lionel pressed his lips together and rolled his eyes.

Jamal gritted his teeth. "Where are they?"

Lionel shook his head, angry with himself. "That kid . . . Samuel . . . he was going to talk with his dad about God. He didn't call us. Judd thought something might have happened. He and Nada—"

"How foolish! I told Judd to stay away from my daughter."

Lionel nodded. "Judd tried to make her stay, but she wouldn't listen."

Jamal grabbed his coat and gloves from the closet and explained to his wife what had happened. She put a hand over her mouth.

"Carpathia says we're free to travel and that no one's a fugitive," Lionel said, "so we don't have anything to worry about."

Jamal glared at him. "If I get my daughter back, you and your friend may leave."

Jamal slammed the door. Lionel grabbed a coat and followed, calling after him, "They took your car!"

"I have another."

"Let me go with you."

"You've caused enough trouble!"

Lionel raced down the stairs behind Jamal. When they made it to the garage, both were out of breath. Lionel helped remove a tarp from the car. The plastic was so cold it snapped.

Jamal tried to start the car but the battery was dead. He dug around in the garage and installed another battery. The car sputtered and coughed, then finally came to life.

"I have to come with you," Lionel said. "You have no idea where Samuel lives."

"Your daring does not impress me. It is my job to keep my daughter safe."

Lionel lowered his voice. "I don't mean any disrespect, sir, but your daughter has a mind of her own. I know what happened to Kasim, and I'm sorry—"

"What does my son have to do with this?"

Lionel shook his head. "Maybe nothing. But maybe you're so scared of losing your other child—"

"I trust God with my family every day," Jamal said. "We risk our lives to protect his servants. We must not take needless chances."

"But just because a person is young," Lionel said, "doesn't mean God can't use him or that his ideas are too dangerous. God wants to use everybody who believes in him."

"Just tell me where this Samuel lives," Jamal said.

"Only if you let me go with you."

Jamal shook his head.

"Come on," Lionel said. "We both want them back. I can help. I'll show you exactly where they went."

Jamal frowned. "No matter what happens, you will leave my home when this is over."

6

Vicki and the other kids at the old school-house were freezing. She believed that those with the mark of the believer would not die from this act of God. The others, who didn't have the mark—Janie, Melinda, and Charlie—looked as cold as she was and stayed as close to the fire as they could.

Melinda moved close to Vicki. Her lips were blue and she trembled. "Are we going to die?"

"I hope not," Vicki said, "but I don't know."

"For somebody who says they know the future, you're not much help."

"We don't know everything that's going to happen," Vicki said, "just what God wants us to know." Vicki put an arm around Melinda. "You don't have to be scared. You can know what's going to happen to you after you die."

"I want to know what's going to happen to me now," Melinda said, "and I want to get warm. Is that asking too much?"

Janie and Charlie scuffled near the fire. They both wanted Phoenix to sleep beside them. Mark separated them and placed Phoenix between them. "Now you see why we asked you to carry all that firewood."

Janie cursed. Mark looked over at Vicki.

"Just leave her alone," Vicki said.

The wind howled through the walls. The generator was dead, so only the fire lit the room.

"We're going to do everything we can to stay alive," Vicki said, "but if you're afraid of dying, why not give your life to God and take care of it forever?"

Melinda pulled the cover up to her chin. "If God gets me out of this, maybe I will."

"Why wait?" Vicki said.

"I'd feel like I was cheating, you know, praying just because I'm in trouble."

"God doesn't care what gets your attention," Vicki said. "All these things—the earthquake, the cold—they're to get to you."

"They've done that."

"Good. Just ask God to forgive you and help you."

Melinda put her head back. "I'm too cold. I can't think." She grew pale. Vicki asked Conrad to help her pull Melinda closer to the fire.

"Just let me sleep," Melinda groaned.

"No way," Vicki said. "Go to sleep when you're this cold and you're dead."

"Fine," Melinda said.

Vicki patted Melinda's face and propped

her against the brick fireplace. Conrad gave Melinda one of his blankets.

Vicki prayed silently. *Please don't let her die.*

As Mr. Goldberg dialed the GC, Judd darted into the room and unplugged the phone.

"You!" the man said.

Judd looked at Samuel and Nada. "You okay?" They nodded. He turned to Mr. Goldberg. "Before you call anyone, listen to your son."

The man raised his eyebrows. "You want *me* to listen?"

"He had the chance to run, but he decided to come back for one more try. He deserves to be heard."

Judd was stunned when Mr. Goldberg sat and said, "Fine." This was too easy.

Samuel looked shocked, but he quickly stood and began. "At the stadium, the final night of the Meeting of the Witnesses, I told you I went to catch the Ben-Judah-ites. That wasn't true. I wanted to know more about God.

"What happened amazed me. People were going forward, falling on their faces. I wanted to go too, but I was scared. I was afraid of what you would say."

"You should have been," his father said.

"When I saw my friends afterward," Samuel said, pointing to Judd, "I knew they would be in trouble. I thought I could save them."

"They are enemies of the Global Community!"

"The more we talked and the more I thought about what the rabbi had said, the more sense it made."

"Nothing that man says makes sense," Mr. Goldberg said. "He is against our leader, the one man who has a plan for this world."

Samuel sat forward, elbows on his knees. "Father, I know now that there is a God and that he loves me. He loves you. He died for us."

"You say this of a god who would take your mother? A god who would allow millions to disappear and millions of others to die in the earthquake and the war?"

"My friends say there are worse things to come," Samuel said, "but this is God's way of calling us."

Mr. Goldberg smirked. "You have peculiar friends. Nicolae Carpathia is my god."

Samuel fell to his knees. "I don't want to disappoint you or disobey you. But I beg you to consider that this may be the truth. On my forehead is the mark of the sealed believer."

"Son, I see nothing on your forehead."

"You cannot see it because you are not one of us."

"Oh, I get it. You have an exclusive club where only the members can detect other members. That would be brilliant if it were true. What does this mark look like?"

Samuel looked at Judd. Judd shook his head. He didn't want anyone knowing the shape of the mark, especially a member of the Global Community.

As Samuel continued, Judd noticed a light blinking on Samuel's father's belt. Why hadn't the man pulled a gun or tried to call the GC again?

Nada jumped into the conversation. "I know all about the Global Community because my brother worked for the potentate."

"I don't care," Mr. Goldberg said. "You have information about the followers of Ben-Judah, and I want that information."

"I would never tell you," she said.

Judd knew something wasn't right. The man was too calm, almost like he was trying to keep the kids talking. A door slammed outside.

Mr. Goldberg smiled. "You didn't think unplugging my phone would keep me from signaling my superiors, did you?" He pulled back his coat to reveal a button. "When I pressed this it was only a matter of time before they got here."

"You shouldn't have come," Samuel told Judd.

Someone pounded on the front door.

TWO

Frostbite

JUDD grabbed Nada and ran for the kitchen. Mr. Goldberg jumped in front of them and Judd blasted into him, sending them both to the floor. Judd tried to get up, but Mr. Goldberg pinned him down.

The front door splintered and a cold wind blew in. "Nada?" came a scream from outside.

"Father!" Nada yelled.

Nada ran to Jamal and hugged him.

"Leave!" Samuel yelled. "The GC will be here soon."

"Come with us," Nada said to Samuel.

Judd flipped over and lay atop Mr. Goldberg, struggling to hold him down.

"Just go, Samuel," Judd yelled, "I can't hold him much longer."

"What about you?" Nada yelled.

Jamal pulled Nada outside. Samuel paused

in the doorway. "Father, I'm sorry. Please consider what I said."

Mr. Goldberg struggled under Judd. "I'll find you, and the rest of them!"

Samuel disappeared, and their car pulled away. Judd let go and scrambled to the kitchen. He unlocked the back door and ran through the alley for the street where he had left Jamal's car.

Will it still be running?

A siren wailed a few blocks away. Judd slipped on the ice and crashed into a row of trash cans. A car pulled away from the curb on the other side of the street. Lionel was behind the wheel.

Judd jumped up and called to him, but Lionel sped away. Judd flailed and shouted, then stopped dead in his tracks. Two GC squad cars slid to a stop, barely missing him.

A man yelled, "Get your hands up!"

Vicki fought to keep Melinda awake and alive. Phoenix whimpered as Janie and Charlie still bickered over who would sleep next to him. Finally, Charlie gave up and let Janie pull Phoenix close. Janie said, "I read a book once where this guy was freezing to death and he used his dog to stay alive. Won't tell you what the guy did, but he had to kill the dog."

Throughout the night Vicki listened to the occasional groan from the kids, the crackling fire, and the whistling wind. At sundown, the wind had seemed to pick up and send the temperature plunging way below zero. Tonight it howled, as if a storm were brewing. Branches from a nearby tree scratched at the windowpane.

Mark scooted close and asked about Melinda. "I can't get her any nearer to the fire without burning her clothes," Vicki said.

"How long will this last?"

Vicki studied Melinda. "I don't think we can take much more and still keep them alive. This fire's all the heat we have."

Mark asked Vicki about Judd and Lionel, then brought up Carl Meninger's mysterious E-mail. Carl had known Mark's cousin John and wanted to meet with Mark. Others questioned whether Carl was a threat to the Young Tribulation Force.

"I have to see him and find out what's up," Mark said, "but I'll make sure we don't meet nearby—"

A thunderous crack interrupted Mark. Glass and snow flew about the room as a branch rammed through the window. Snow gushed in, dousing the fire instantly with a loud hiss.

The kids were plunged into total darkness.

Lionel hated the thought of leaving Judd, but Jamal had ordered him. Lionel waited as long as he could, but when he saw the lights of the GC squad car, he hit the accelerator and sped away.

Lionel had never driven a car alone. He had backed out of Judd's driveway a few times just for grins, but this was different. A wave of relief swept over him when he finally arrived at Jamal's house. When he had the car safely sheltered, he trudged upstairs.

Jamal scolded Nada, but she didn't back down. "What would you have done if a friend said they were going to call and didn't?" she said.

"Go," Jamal said, pointing to her room, "I don't want to hear it."

"You treat me like a child," Nada said.

"You act like one, I treat you like one."

"Sir, she was just trying to protect me," Samuel said.

Jamal stared at the boy. "I am glad you have become a true believer in Jesus, your Messiah. However, that does not excuse my daughter's disobedience."

Nada came into the room again, her hands clasped in front of her. "Father, you know how much I love you. I want to obey you, and I'll admit I made a mistake."

"It could have cost your life," Jamal said.

"Yes, but it is *my* life. I have to make decisions on my own."

Lionel paced the floor. "Let's focus on Judd right now, okay? What are they going to do with him?"

Samuel shrugged. "They'll take him to headquarters and question him."

"And he will lead them directly here," Jamal said.

Lionel sighed. "Judd won't do that."

"Don't you remember what the GC did to your friend Mr. Stein?" Jamal said. "They only let him go because they thought he was dead!"

"Wait," Lionel said, "what about the potentate's order? Won't they have to let him go?"

"What order?" Nada said, poking her head back into the room. "We didn't hear anything."

Lionel explained that Nicolae Carpathia had tried to bargain with the witnesses, Eli and Moishe, at the Wailing Wall. When the two witnesses stopped talking, Carpathia had cleared the Trib Force of any wrongdoing. "He also said nobody who agrees with the teachings of Dr. Ben-Judah is considered a fugitive or an enemy of the Global Community. Believers are supposed to be able to travel and do what any other citizen can do."

"That means they'll release Judd," Nada said.

"What the potentate says in front of the cameras and what happens in a Global Community jail cell are two different things," Jamal said.

"What if we reach him?" Nada said.

Lionel looked at Samuel. "Know anyone you can trust who works with your father?"

Samuel pursed his lips. "A lieutenant who knew my mother might—"

Jamal interrupted. "It is too great a risk. You will not make the call from here."

"What are we supposed to do?" Lionel said. "We have to let Judd know—"

"Pray that God will intervene," Jamal said.

Vicki yelled, "Is anyone hurt?"

"My leg's broken!" Janie screamed. But when the kids moved the branch, Janie only had a scratch.

Conrad found an old newspaper in the next room, lit a match, and set the paper on fire. The wind blew it out. He stepped into the hallway and lit it again. "Grab anything that will keep you warm and follow me!" Conrad yelled.

Vicki helped Melinda to her feet. Flakes of ice clung to the girl's eyebrows and she shivered violently.

Phoenix bounded away from Janie and down the stairs toward Conrad. "It's gonna be colder down there than it is up here!" Janie whined.

Mark helped Charlie to his feet, and they stumbled down the stairs. Vicki hated to admit it but Janie was right. As they moved farther underground, the temperature fell.

"Trust me," Conrad said.

Vicki was the last through the underground entrance. She closed the door. The icy wind no longer whipped at her clothes, but she could barely stand the freezing cold.

Conrad and Mark brought wood stored in the tunnel and piled it on the earthen floor. "If we can get a fire going, the wind won't be able to blow it out."

Janie picked an icicle off the side of a wall. "We're all going to wind up human Popsicles."

"Stop it," Vicki said.

"At least there aren't snakes and bugs," Shelly said.

Vicki bundled Melinda in blankets and rubbed the girl's arms and shoulders.

"I can't feel my feet," Melinda said.

Smoke filled the room when the fire started. The kids gasped for air. Conrad opened the entrance to the tunnel. "This will work as a flue."

Smoke floated through the opening, and the kids breathed easier. "It's going to take a while to warm up," Conrad said.

In the corner, Darrion and Shelly prayed softly. Janie cornered Phoenix again and dragged him as close to the fire as he would go.

While Mark stoked the fire, Conrad joined Vicki. "This is the only place I could think of. Any other spot in the house and we'd burn the place down."

Vicki nodded. "It was good thinking."

"I'm sorry about turning off the generator—"

"You were trying to conserve energy. It's not your fault."

"I keep thinking about Eli and Moishe. I wish we could have seen what happened. Do you think they killed Carpathia?"

Vicki shook her head. "It's not his time yet. Tsion says the witnesses will die before Nicolae. I just hope God puts a stop to this judgment soon."

Melinda moaned and complained about her feet. Vicki carefully pulled the covers back and helped take off her shoes and socks. The right foot was pale but looked okay. When Vicki took off Melinda's left shoe she gasped. Three of her toes were turning a dark blue.

"That's frostbite," Conrad whispered.

Judd sat in an interrogation room at the Global Community precinct. Only a few officers were at their desks when he was brought in from the cold. He rubbed his wrists where the icy handcuffs had been. *At least the station is warm,* he thought.

Judd hoped Nada and the others had gotten away without being seen. He wondered whether the GC would track them down. He kicked himself for putting Nada in that situation and resolved that no matter what the GC did to him he would never tell them about Jamal's apartment building.

Judd's thoughts turned to the kids in Illinois. What would Vicki say about this? Judd figured she had the generator going and the schoolhouse warm. He smiled.

Without thinking, Judd began to pray. It was as natural as breathing. Just speak to

God. He knew the Bible said believers should pray continually. That was something his mother had quoted when he was younger. He had laughed at her. He used to think it meant you had to be in a church service your entire life. Now he knew it meant just giving your thoughts and concerns to God.

Judd asked God to give him the right words to say to the GC. As he prayed, he wondered if God had placed him in the hands of the Global Community for a reason. His friend Pete had talked about God to a GC officer. It was a stretch, but there might be someone here who needed to hear the truth.

A man entered the interrogation room, then quickly retreated, leaving the door open. A nearby television showed a report about the two witnesses and Potentate Carpathia. Judd couldn't believe what Nicolae was saying about the Trib Force and the followers of Tsion Ben-Judah.

Mr. Goldberg entered with a tall man. Judd looked down at the small wooden table and shifted in his seat. The tall man rifled through papers, then stared at Judd. When he spoke, Judd thought he recognized the voice, but he couldn't place it.

"I am Deputy Commander Woodruff," the man said, looking at Judd's fake papers. He read the information aloud and said, "Is that correct?"

Judd stared at the man.

"Are you a follower of Ben-Judah?"

"Have the things the rabbi has predicted come true?" Judd said.

Deputy Commander Woodruff folded his arms.

"Even the brilliant Chaim Rosenzweig has said we should look to the rabbi for wisdom," Judd said, "so I guess the answer is yes."

Mr. Goldberg jumped from his chair. "You'll be sorry you talked that way!"

The deputy commander calmed Mr. Goldberg and turned to Judd. "We have reason to believe you know where Ben-Judah is hiding. If that is the case, we will get the information from you."

Judd leaned close and lowered his voice. "Why would you need to know the hiding place of someone who is not wanted by the Global Community?"

Woodruff frowned. Judd repeated what he had heard Nicolae Carpathia say on the news report. "I'd say you are in direct violation of an order given by the potentate himself. And if those two witnesses at the Wailing Wall hear you're holding someone simply because

I agree with the rabbi, things are going to stay cold for a long time."

The two men stepped outside. "I didn't hear that the potentate had lifted—," Mr. Goldberg said as they closed the door. A few minutes later a guard escorted Judd back to his cell.

THREE

God's Thaw

VICKI helped Melinda through the night. Mark had learned first aid in the militia and grabbed a pot from the kitchen to melt snow. When the water was warm, he soaked Melinda's foot and rubbed the darkened toes.

"Can't make this water too hot or it'll hurt her," Mark said.

When Melinda moaned, Vicki found aspirin in a bottle and gave her a drink. When morning came, Melinda's toes were blistered but she could move them slightly.

"Normal," Mark said. "The color looks better. We have to make sure they don't freeze again."

While Melinda, Charlie, and Janie huddled by the fire downstairs, the others headed upstairs. The kids removed the tree limb and nailed boards over the windows.

"That should keep the wind out," Conrad said.

While Darrion and Shelly built another fire, Conrad and Mark inspected the generator. Vicki found the canned food, but it was frozen. She placed several opened cans of soup directly on the fire. When the soup was warm, Vicki brought it downstairs. Janie complained but wolfed it down and asked for more.

Melinda wore four pairs of socks and shivered under several blankets. "What's going to happen to us?" she said.

Vicki patted her shoulder. "We'll take care of you."

Lionel and Samuel prayed for Samuel's father and Judd. Nada and the rest of her family remained behind closed doors. Late in the morning, Lionel heard a report from the Wailing Wall. The two witnesses, Eli and Moishe, had spoken out against the Global Community again.

"Woe to the leaders who make promises but do not do what they say," Eli wailed. "The eyes of the Lord watch over those who do right; his ears are open to their cries for help. But the Lord turns his face against those who do evil; he will erase their memory from the earth."

Moishe picked up the message. "This judgment shall not pass until those who are sealed are released from their bondage."

Vicki found Mark and Conrad working on the generator. The sun was out, but the light was weak and the temperature hadn't risen much. The two blew into cupped hands to stay warm.

Mark shook his head. "This line won't thaw anytime soon."

When they were back inside, Conrad asked about Melinda's foot.

"It blistered some more and she's in a lot of pain," Vicki said, "but I guess that's good."

Mark nodded. "If we can, let's get her back up here so—"

"Already done," Vicki said. "Charlie and Janie, too."

Vicki led them to the three, who were huddled close to the fire. Janie held tightly to Phoenix. The room flickered in the firelight.

"How much wood do we have left?" Vicki whispered.

"We've gone through it faster than I thought," Mark said. "If we stick with one fire, we might be able to keep this room warm for another week or so."

Judd's cell was chilly, but he wasn't affected by the cold like some of the other prisoners. They moaned and cried for more blankets. One man hadn't moved in hours. When guards carried him out on a stretcher, Judd realized he was dead.

On Friday evening Judd noticed a flurry of activity in the jail area. Several times a guard walked near Judd's cell to check on him. Finally, Judd was led to a room where Mr. Goldberg met him.

The man fidgeted with a pink piece of paper. "We have reviewed your file—"

"You have no reason to hold me," Judd interrupted. "The potentate said followers of Rabbi Ben-Judah are free to move around."

"The deputy commander has spoken with New Babylon about the meaning of the potentate's statement."

"The meaning?" Judd said. "Seemed pretty clear to me. I've done nothing wrong."

Mr. Goldberg leaned close. "You have taken my son away from me. You brainwashed him with your religion. You are a dangerous young man."

Judd paused. Instead of hating the man, he felt pity. "My parents and my whole family were taken in the disappearances. Before that, my mom and dad tried to get me to go to church and listen to the same things your son believes. I wish I'd listened to them. I wish *you'd* listen. You don't have to be separated from your son or from God."

A guard opened the door and motioned for the man. Mr. Goldberg left. A half hour later, Judd was returned to his cell.

Later that night, Judd noticed an older, dark-skinned man in the next cell. The grizzled man scooted his cot close to the bars and said, "American?"

Judd was cautious but moved closer. "Yeah."

"I tell you something important. In return, you give me blanket."

"What could you possibly tell me that—"

"You get out soon," the man said. "Heard it from guard. But I tell you something else. First, blanket."

Judd folded a blanket and shoved it through the bars.

The old man wrapped it tightly around him. "When you leave before, guard came. Take coat from bed."

"They took my coat?" Judd said. "What would they want with—"

"They bring it back. Did something to it."

Judd felt his coat. Nothing was different. "What would they have done?"

The man shrugged. "Heard something else. You must be important person."

"Why?"

"New Babylon say you get released. Others like you."

Judd nodded and told the old man about Rabbi Ben-Judah. The man turned and pulled the covers over him when Judd explained the message of the gospel.

"No God," the man mumbled.

Judd tried again, but the man yelled and others nearby awoke. Judd thought about what the man had told him. If the GC had planted a tracking device somewhere in his coat, he would lead them straight to Jamal and the others. Later in the night, Judd woke the old man and proposed an even exchange: the old man's coat for Judd's. "All you have to do is keep quiet about the coat for a few hours."

The man handed him an old coat about the same color as Judd's. Judd wrapped it around his shoulders and fell asleep.

The next morning keys jangled Judd awake. He could see his breath in the frosty jail. A guard opened the door and motioned Judd outside.

Judd stood up. "What's going on?"

"Bring your coat," the guard said. "You're free to go."

The guard led Judd to the front of the station, where he signed for his wallet and fake ID. Judd shoved them into a pocket.

Judd looked around for Mr. Goldberg or the deputy commander. Neither was in sight. Outside the station he quickly pulled out his ID and money and threw the wallet in a nearby trash can. If there was a transmitter in his coat, they might have planted one in his wallet as well.

Judd ran a few blocks until he came to a familiar street name. He was at least an hour's walk from Jamal's apartment building. He passed several bodies of those who had frozen to death.

Judd ducked into a crowded coffee shop and sat on a stool by the window. As he sipped a warm drink, he listened to the conversations around him. People spoke of the cold and the two crazy men here in Jerusalem. A few minutes later, as Judd suspected, GC squad cars raced past. He stood up and pushed his way to the front. Before he could get to the door, something stopped him in his tracks.

The sun.

At 10:30 A.M. Jerusalem time, the bright, yellow sun appeared. People who had been inside for weeks ran into the streets and lifted their faces toward the sky. Crowds blocked traffic, but no one seemed to mind. The earth had broken out of its icy spell.

A monitor inside the coffee shop showed a replay of the entire conversation between Nicolae and the two witnesses. Commentators praised the work of the potentate. Judd smiled. He knew God had been looking out for him and other believers.

Early Saturday morning, Vicki awoke and noticed something different. She stumbled to the kitchen. Brilliant sunshine streamed through the windows. She let out a whoop, and the other kids came running.

Mark and Conrad quickly got to work on the generator. The others helped pull food from the frozen storage area. Melinda stayed inside with her foot still wrapped. Color had returned to her toes, and Mark thought she would be okay in a few days.

Vicki boiled drinking water and thawed enough food for dinner. She wanted to resume classes on Monday and had planned a worship service to celebrate the end of the judgment.

Vicki noticed Janie was missing. She found her walking by the river. Vicki wanted to scold the girl or punish her in some way but decided to let it go.

"I'm glad that's over," Janie said. "Feels like spring again."

"It's not over," Vicki said.

"You mean it's going to get cold again?"

Vicki shook her head. "The judgments get worse and worse. That's part of what we're learning in our classes. See, God wants us to come to him now while there's—"

Janie patted Vicki on the shoulder and interrupted. "Just wait. When the guys get the computer working, I'll bet it shows Nicolae had something to do with getting things back on track."

Judd walked into the crowded streets and made his way toward Jamal's hiding place. He watched for any sign of a Global Community squad car. Once, a siren blared behind him and Judd darted into an alley. Later, he found they were headed to an accident scene.

Judd waited near Jamal's building until

dusk, scanning the street for anyone suspicious. When he was sure no one was watching, he slipped into the underground garage and found the back entrance. He knocked on Jamal's door. Someone opened the peephole and closed it. A few seconds later, Lionel let Judd in.

"Man, it's good to see you," Lionel said, leading Judd to his room. Samuel greeted Judd.

Judd told them his story. Samuel quizzed him about his father.

"He seems closed to the truth, at least for now," Judd said.

"I've been praying for him ever since I received the mark of the believer," Samuel said. "I don't understand."

"It took you a while to come around," Judd said. "Maybe it's just going to take time."

Lionel took Judd aside and apologized for not waiting at Samuel's house. "I didn't have a choice. Jamal said I had to follow him closely or he wouldn't let me in the garage."

"What about Nada?"

"Basically he's keeping her locked up," Lionel said. "Samuel and I have been working with people in the building since the sun came out. We've been helping Jamal get them back into their apartments, but the guy is as cold as ice toward us."

"Doesn't he know it was Nada's idea to—"

"Doesn't matter," Lionel said. "He blames you for what happened. He said she could have been killed."

Judd shuddered. "It could have been a lot worse, but everything turned out okay."

Lionel pulled out a sealed envelope. "I don't think so. I haven't seen Nada since we got here. She slipped this note under my door last night. She said to make sure you got it when you returned."

Judd opened the envelope and scanned the note.

> Judd,
> Remember when you asked me if I had feelings for you? I said I didn't, but that wasn't the truth. Lionel was right. Since you came, my feelings for you have increased. I pray you see this note and that we will be able to talk soon. Don't let my father scare you. Please write me as soon as you can.
> Love,
> Nada

Judd handed the note to Lionel. Lionel read it and shook his head.

"Don't say it," Judd said.

"Man, I told you—"

Judd grabbed the note and stuck it in his pocket. "I don't need that right now."

The door opened and Jamal stepped in. His face was grim. "I have made a difficult decision. Your presence here is not good for my family. I will have to ask you to leave."

"Can't we talk about this?" Judd said.

Jamal held up a hand. "I have made my decision."

FOUR

Nada's Secret

Vicki and the others were amazed by how fast the snow melted. The river rose just as quickly. Conrad sealed the outside entrance to the underground tunnel. Shelly asked if they should move to higher ground.

"It would have to rise another ten feet before we'd have to move," Mark said.

The generator finally began working late Saturday night. Mark checked their E-mail messages. There was nothing from Judd or Lionel, but he did find two messages from Carl Meninger. Mark opened the first, the one he had been reading when the computer had gone dead.

Carl wrote that he had been released from the hospital in South Carolina and was ready to visit Mark. "I'll take a military transport and get as close to Chicago as I can. Just give me the word."

Mark opened the second E-mail, which had been written the night before. "I want to take a flight soon, but I haven't heard from you," Carl wrote. "Are you still alive? Has something happened? Please contact me as soon as possible." Carl included a phone number at the bottom of the E-mail.

Mark picked up the phone, but Conrad stopped him. "I still don't like this," Conrad said. "I know you want to hear about John, but this might be a GC trap."

"I told you I was going to be careful," Mark said. "I'll drive a cycle to meet him somewhere away from here. Maybe Indiana."

"I think it's a good idea," Vicki said. "If this guy Carl isn't on the level, Mark can find out and get away."

Mark dialed the number and asked for Carl. He went into the next room to talk and returned in a few minutes.

"Carl's not there," Mark said. "His roommate said he took a transport flight early this morning. He thought something had happened and wanted to find me."

"Just what we need," Conrad said, "the GC looking for our hideout."

"Did he say where he was headed?" Vicki said.

Mark shook his head. "It could take him a while and a few different planes to get close.

One thing's for sure, he's not coming to Chicago."

"Why not?" Vicki said.

"There are reports of big-time radiation downtown," Mark said.

Vicki gasped. "Nuclear?"

Conrad scratched his head. "I don't remember Chicago getting hit with any nukes."

"Whether they did or didn't isn't the point," Mark said. "The GC and everybody else are staying as far away from it as they can." Mark typed a response on E-mail. "Carl's supposed to check this every day."

"What are you telling him?" Vicki said.

"As soon as he gets close, I'm on my way."

Judd, Lionel, and Samuel ate breakfast Sunday morning and waited.

Samuel talked about his father and the possibility of seeing him again. "I want you to call me Sam. It's what my friends call me."

Lionel brought Judd up to date on the warming center Jamal had set up downstairs. "A lot of those people seem interested in learning more," Lionel said, "but Jamal is cautious. He doesn't want to alert the GC."

Jamal's wife brought them food and gave

Judd a pained look when he tried to talk
with her.

"We don't have money," Judd said. "Where
are we supposed to go?"

Jamal's wife shook her head but didn't
speak.

Judd wrote a quick note to the kids in Illinois. He explained their situation, leaving
out the part about Nada.

"What are we going to do when he kicks us
out?" Lionel said.

"He can't kick us out," Judd said.

Sam said, "You have to understand how
important family is to Jamal. You have
offended him."

"But we're spiritual brothers," Judd said.

"True," Sam said, "and I'm new to this so I
don't understand everything, but you have
offended him. You have come between him
and his daughter. That is not good."

Judd felt helpless. Since the disappearances
he had been a take-charge person. When a
problem came up, he solved it. Sometimes
not the best way, but he acted. Now he was
at the mercy of someone else. Someone who
didn't trust him.

"You have to tell me," Lionel said when he
got Judd alone. "Do you have feelings for
Nada?"

Judd looked down. "I don't know. I mean,

she's easy to talk to. I like her as a friend. She's got a heart for God—"

"And she's a knockout," Lionel added, "but that has nothing to do with it."

Judd blushed. "Jamal has been good to us. I can't go against him. Besides, I don't think this is the time to start a romance."

"Especially when there's someone waiting back in the States."

"What do you mean?" Judd said.

Lionel frowned. "You know exactly what and who I mean. Vicki."

"No way," Judd said, "we fight too much."

"You're different from her," Lionel said. "You're supposed to be."

Judd put a finger to his lips. Voices in the next room. The phone rang. Lots of activity.

"I've got a feeling we're moving," Lionel said. "And you'd better write a note to Nada."

Vicki and the others were up early Sunday morning. Mark packed food and a change of clothes and checked on the motorcycles. Only one worked since the freeze. The rest of the morning was spent preparing for the worship service. The kids didn't know many songs, but they typed up the ones they knew and put them on the computer screen.

They took turns reading verses from the Bible and telling what God was teaching them. Melinda and Charlie seemed to listen closely. Janie sighed a lot and stared out the window.

When it was Vicki's turn, she pulled up news coverage the kids hadn't seen. "I got up early to find out what happened with Nicolae and the witnesses. Carpathia made a deal and promised safety for those who believe the message of Tsion Ben-Judah."

"So it was Nicolae that made it happen," Janie said.

Vicki smiled. "He may have made a deal, but it was God who lifted the judgment from us."

Janie rolled her eyes.

Vicki pulled out a sheet of paper. "I found something interesting on Tsion's Web site this morning. It proves my point that we have a lot to learn from the Bible, but we also have to be students of what's happening around us. Tsion says the next judgment from God will be the most dramatic yet."

"How could it get more dramatic than a worldwide earthquake?" Darrion said.

"I'll read you what Tsion says," Vicki said. "'Because of the proven truth of Luke 21, I urge all, believers and unbelievers alike, to train your eyes on the skies. I believe this is the message from the two witnesses.'"

"I don't get it," Shelly said.

Vicki pulled up the computer video of the Meeting of the Witnesses. Tsion Ben-Judah cleared his throat and began. "This passage warns that once the earth has been darkened by a third, three terrible woes will follow. These are particularly ominous, so much so that they will be announced from heaven in advance."

Vicki moved the video forward and said, "We've just been through that judgment. Now Eli and Moishe come up from behind him and read the Scripture Tsion had picked out."

Vicki's voice caught when she saw the two prophets standing directly behind Tsion. It was like watching something from a biblical movie, only this was real.

Moishe recited the text without looking at a Bible. "'And I beheld, and heard an angel flying through the midst of heaven, saying with a loud voice, Woe, woe, woe, to the inhabiters of the earth by reason of the other voices of the trumpet of the three angels, which are yet to sound!'"

Vicki paused the clip.

"What does all that mean?" Melinda said.

"It means you don't want to wait another minute to make your decision about God," Shelly said. "This next thing that's coming is going to be awful."

"You're just trying to scare us," Janie said.

Melinda looked hard at Janie. "I don't think so. They've been right about everything so far."

Judd gave Sam the note and asked him to slip it under Nada's door when no one was looking. Sam returned, shaking his head. Jamal walked in behind him.

"Come with me," Jamal said.

"Do you want us to get our stuff together?" Lionel said.

Jamal turned. "Just follow me."

"Wait," Judd said. "Before we go I'd like to speak with your daughter."

Jamal stared at Judd.

"I know how you feel," Judd said, "but this might be my last chance to talk with her."

Jamal opened the door to Nada's room and called her. Nada walked out, her head down. "Two minutes," he said sternly.

Judd looked at Sam and Lionel. The two walked into the hallway.

"I got your note," Judd said.

"It was foolish of me," Nada said. "I
should never—"

"It was sweet," Judd said. "You're so easy
to talk to. It was like instant friendship
between us."

"But you don't feel the same for me?"
Nada said, finally looking at Judd. Nada had
deep brown eyes, and brown hair that
touched her shoulders.

"I don't know how I feel, especially if your
dad is making us go away," Judd said.

"I'll go with you," Nada said.

"We only have a minute," Judd said. "I just
wanted to let you know I care about you. I'm
not sure if this goes deeper than friendship
or not, or if this is the time to—"

"You don't have to say anything more,"
Nada interrupted.

"Please," Judd said, "I want you as part
of the Young Trib Force no matter what
happens."

"How can you hope to fight the Global
Community when you won't even stand up
to my father?"

Judd rubbed his forehead. "Right now the
best thing for me to do is honor your father's
wishes. Then, at some point, I hope—"

"Go," Nada said. "Just go."

Nada turned and retreated to her room,

crying. Jamal took him by the arm and led him into the hall.

"You will have no further contact with her," Jamal said.

Judd didn't argue. He followed the others to the small car and got in the backseat. They stopped at a house that looked familiar. When the front door opened, Judd realized it was the home of Yitzhak, the man who had first helped them when they had arrived in Jerusalem. Yitzhak warmly greeted them, hugged Sam tightly, and ushered them into the dimly lit living room.

A bearded man sat in the shadows. His face seemed to glow.

"It is good to see you," the man said.

"Mr. Stein?" Lionel said, moving closer.

"Yes, it is me," Mr. Stein said, and he hugged Judd and Lionel. Judd introduced Sam and told Mr. Stein what had happened with Sam's father.

Mr. Stein put a hand on Sam's shoulder. "We will be your family now. Perhaps your father will come around. We will leave that to God."

"Would you speak with him, sir?" Sam said.

"When the chance comes, I will speak with him."

Mr. Stein asked them to sit. "My time away

was incredible. Yitzhak and I were up until all hours of the night studying, praying. I would wake up after only two or three hours of sleep and be ready to go again."

Yitzhak laughed. "I wanted to give him sleeping pills."

"Were you affected by the cold?" Lionel said.

Mr. Stein smiled. "It was like living in a refrigerator, but God kept our hearts warm. He has confirmed to me that I am one of his witnesses. I believe I have been given a special mission."

Judd looked at Yitzhak. Had Mr. Stein gone over the edge? "What kind of mission?"

"In our cabin was a huge map of the world," Mr. Stein said. "I was drawn to it. I kept looking at the different countries, wondering what God was saying to me.

"I believe God has selected me to travel to a group of people I have never heard of and have never seen."

"What?" Judd said.

"I prayed in front of that map every day. Sometimes for hours. Last night I had a dream. I was floating toward the ground. A huge desert stretched before me. And then, I saw a river, and people, hundreds of them, thousands who had no contact with the outside world.

"They wore strange clothing and talked in a language I have never heard. I asked, 'Who are these people?' I sensed I was being called to tell them the gospel."

"What country is it?" Lionel said.

Mr. Stein smiled. "I don't know. I can only surmise it is somewhere in Africa. I am leaving tomorrow."

"What?" Judd said. "How are you going to go if you don't know what country they're in? How will you talk without an interpreter? A trip like that could take weeks, even months."

Mr. Stein stroked his beard. "I gave my word to God that I would make myself available. If this is what he wants me to do, I know he will make the way clear to me."

"The GC took all your cash!" Judd said. "How will you—"

"I have some," Yitzhak said. "It should be enough to at least get you there."

"Wait," Judd said. "You need to plan this better."

"I do not know how much longer before the next judgment," Mr. Stein said. "I must go as soon as possible."

Jamal looked at Mr. Stein. "There is one other thing, correct?"

"Oh yes," Mr. Stein said. "In the vision I was not alone. There was someone beside me the whole time."

"Who?" Lionel said.

Mr. Stein turned. "It was you, Judd. I believe God wants you to come with me."

FIVE

Incredible Faith

JUDD blinked. It was one thing for Mr. Stein to go off the deep end, but another to drag him along. "You want me to go?" Judd said.

Mr. Stein turned to Jamal. "I understand from Yitzhak that my friends have caused trouble in your home."

Jamal looked at the floor. "My daughter won't speak to me. My wife is upset. I am in a difficult position."

"If you will care for Lionel and Samuel while we are gone, I promise to take full responsibility when I return."

"And when would that be?" Jamal said.

Mr. Stein sighed. "I do not even know where I am going, much less when I will return. I suppose we could find another—"

"No," Jamal said, "leave them with me. Before we came here I heard about an important job. I think they can help." He put out his hand. "We will pray for your safety and that God will be glorified through this."

"Thank you," Mr. Stein said. He turned to Judd. "Are you willing to go?"

Judd closed his eyes and breathed a prayer. "If this is really what God wants you to do, and I'm supposed to be part of it, I'll go."

Judd slept at Yitzhak's home and awakened early the next day. Though Nicolae Carpathia had promised that believers in Christ could move about freely, they didn't want to take any chances. Mr. Stein had his photo taken, and a new, fake passport was made for him.

Monday afternoon they pooled the money they needed and traveled to the airport. Yitzhak drove Mr. Stein and Judd and hugged them both.

"May you have great success!" Yitzhak shouted over the roar of a jet engine.

Judd and Mr. Stein waved and walked through the GC security.

Monday morning in Illinois, Vicki set up the room for the first day of classes since the judgment. Melinda hobbled into the room and put her foot on a chair. "Figured I'd get here early to get a good seat," Melinda said.

Conrad came into the room, shaking his head.

"What's up?" Vicki said.

"It's that safe I found in the bell tower," Conrad said. "I poured water in the lock and left it outside in the cold. Thought the freeze might bust it. Nothing. I've drilled a hole in the lock, tried to saw it off. It simply won't open."

"Forget the lock and work on the box," Melinda said.

"It's solid steel," Conrad said. "This thing was made more than a hundred years ago, and it was made to last."

Vicki counted heads as the others came into the room. "Where's Janie?"

"I saw her after breakfast," Shelly said. "Said she was going for a walk to meditate."

"Okay," Vicki said, "we'd better get started."

Vicki pulled together material from Tsion Ben-Judah's Web site. She also included much of the daytime teaching the kids had recorded from the Meeting of the Witnesses.

When lunchtime came, the kids took a break. Mark checked for a message from Carl but found none. While the others ate, he went outside. A few minutes later he returned out of breath and took Vicki aside. "Janie's not back, and I've looked all around the house and by the river."

"This is her choice," Vicki said. "I can't

make her study with us. Besides, the class went better without her. Charlie and Melinda are actually paying attention."

"That's not the point," Mark said. "What if she wanders off and the GC find her?"

"We can't baby-sit her—"

"But she could lead them back here," Mark said. "You know she'd trade her freedom for a chance to watch some music videos."

Vicki stared out the window. She had known it would be a risk allowing Janie into the schoolhouse. She had hoped the girl would be a believer by now.

"I feel like this is my responsibility," Mark said. "I was the one who brought her here."

"You and Conrad look for her," Vicki said. "We'll do chores the rest of the afternoon."

"Maybe she's just on some rock, chanting to Nicolae," Mark said, "but I'd feel better if we found her."

Lionel was cautious around Jamal the next day. Finally he decided to talk with the man. When the two were alone Lionel said, "I know you don't like what happened with Judd and Nada, but I have to know if that's going to affect us."

"I have no hard feelings for you personally," Jamal said. "If you become a father someday, perhaps you will understand."

After the conversation it seemed like a weight was lifted from the house. Nada came out of her room and talked. Jamal's wife appeared less upset, and the conversations seemed lighter.

Sam asked how to talk about God with others. Lionel showed him transcripts from Tsion's messages. Before long, Sam asked to set up a meeting with his father.

"Let's take it slowly right now," Lionel said.

"But Tsion says the next judgment could come at any time."

"I know," Lionel said, "but let's give your father time to cool off."

Monday afternoon, after Jamal had dropped off Judd's clothes at Yitzhak's house, Jamal took Lionel, Sam, and Nada to an empty warehouse on the outskirts of Jerusalem. "This is the important job I spoke about last night," he said. He put a finger to his lips and knocked on the door four times. There was a faint sound of a machine running inside. It stopped, but no one came to the door. Jamal led them inside. The metal door clanged shut behind them.

The room was nearly empty and eerily quiet. Jamal grabbed one end of a desk that sat in the middle of the room. Lionel and Sam took the other end, and they slid it toward the wall.

Jamal bent down and lifted what looked like a paperweight on the floor. Lionel gasped. There was modern printing equipment, and a dozen workers were packing small boxes in the basement. The workers were of different nationalities, but all had the mark of the true believer.

Jamal hugged one of the men leading the operation. They talked in a different language. Lionel scanned the boxes. "Property of the Global Community" was printed on the side. Lionel looked in an open box and saw pamphlets. The stack was printed in weird characters, like Chinese. The next set of pamphlets was printed in Spanish. Another in French. Lionel had taken a semester of French and recognized words from the Bible.

"It's all stuff about God," Sam said, picking up a stack printed in Hebrew.

Jamal introduced the kids. "The material in this room will be sent around the world."

"How?" Lionel said.

"With the help of the Global Community," Jamal said.

"What?" Sam said. "They would never—"

"They don't know we're sending it," the leader explained. "These boxes all go to the airport. Some people on the inside sneak it onto the Condor 216."

Lionel's mouth opened wide. "You mean Carpathia's plane?"

"Christian literature is flooding the globe, and the potentate has no idea it's his own plane spreading it!" Jamal said.

Judd was amazed at the busy airport. The freezing temperatures had grounded most flights. Now, hundreds of people were trying to get out of Israel. Judd looked at the monitors for flights to the U.S. Many big cities like Chicago weren't listed.

"Which airline?" Judd asked Mr. Stein.

Mr. Stein looked at the row of ticket agents. "We need to find someone who can be used by God."

Judd shook his head. "We don't know where we're going or if we have enough money to get there. People back home would call me crazy if I did this."

"Yitzhak explained it this way," Mr. Stein said. "These are incredible days when we must have incredible faith in an incredible God. Following the Rapture, God is showing his miraculous ability in new ways. Don't underestimate the power and the love of the

Almighty. He cares for the people we're going to."

"I believe that. I just wish we knew more."

"Faith means taking one step at a time," Mr. Stein said. "If we knew the whole plan, we might trust in ourselves or become scared."

Mr. Stein had come a long way in a short time. It seemed only a few weeks ago that he had been so against his daughter, Chaya, and her belief in Jesus.

They chose a counter with only a few people in line. When it was their turn, the ticket agent smiled and asked if they needed to check baggage.

"We simply need two tickets," Mr. Stein said.

The agent entered their information. "Destination?"

"We're not sure."

"Excuse me?"

Mr. Stein smiled. "This is rather difficult to explain. But I think there's a desert nearby."

The agent stared. "You're kidding." She looked at Judd. "He's kidding, right?"

Judd shook his head. "He's serious."

"I know what the people look like, what they wear, and that—"

"Sir, we're very busy. Why don't you figure

out where you need to go and then come
back—"

"Africa," Mr. Stein said.

"Africa," the agent said. "That's a conti-
nent. I need a city."

Mr. Stein scratched his beard. "Is there
someone who could help, a pilot or a
manager?"

People lined up behind Judd. Some
shoved suitcases forward with their feet and
sighed. Someone said, "This guy is loony."

The ticket agent took a deep breath. "You
said there was a desert nearby? The biggest
desert in Africa is the Sahara, so we're probably talking about northern Africa."

"Very good," Mr. Stein said, "now we're
getting somewhere."

"The Sahara is three million square miles,
sir. We're not even close."

Judd spotted a man in uniform talking
with a baggage handler. He had the mark of
the believer on his forehead. "Perhaps that
man could help us," Judd said.

The agent shook her head. "That's my
boss; he's much too busy—"

"What's his name?" Mr. Stein said.

"Mr. Isaacs is in charge of all the daily—"

"Mr. Isaacs!" Mr. Stein yelled. "Please,
come help us!"

There was more grumbling behind Judd as Mr. Isaacs slowly walked forward. He was stocky, in his late forties, and had a round face. He smiled when he saw that Judd and Mr. Stein were believers.

"Is there a problem, Vivian?" Mr. Isaacs said.

The agent spoke through clenched teeth. "These gentlemen want a ticket but don't know where they're going."

"Let me take them down here," Mr. Isaacs said, motioning Mr. Stein and Judd to an empty spot. The man hit a few keys, then shook hands with Judd and Mr. Stein. "How can I help?"

Mr. Stein explained his dream and their need to leave as soon as possible.

Mr. Isaacs studied the monitor. "We're definitely talking northern Africa. My guess is west of the Sahara." He pulled up an on-screen map and turned the monitor so Judd and Mr. Stein could see. The man pointed to lines on the screen.

"This area is known as the 10/40 window. Many people who have not responded to the gospel live between ten and forty degrees latitude. Missionaries had broken through to the area before the Rapture, but there are still people who haven't heard."

"That is why God is sending me," Mr. Stein said.

"And others like you," Mr. Isaacs said. "We've had about a dozen witnesses looking for flights to remote areas in the last few days, but no one to this specific area. It's incredible what God is doing."

Mr. Stein described the people in his dream.

Mr. Isaacs nodded as he listened and pulled up a smaller map. "I've heard of nomads in this area, taking their flocks wherever they can find food and water."

"How could they have survived the recent cold?" Mr. Stein said.

"Good question," Mr. Isaacs said. He punched in some data and pointed to a small dot in a country called Mali. "We can fly you into the capital, Bamako, but from there you'll have to find a way into the countryside. Maybe a chartered flight or a Land Rover could get you to those people."

Mr. Stein pulled out a wad of cash. The cost of the ticket was more than they had. "How much for two tickets?"

Mr. Isaacs smiled. "But you have come on the very day we're offering a discount. I'll make up the rest of the money."

"We couldn't let you—"

Mr. Isaacs leaned over the counter. "It is a privilege to be involved in some small way in God's work. Don't take this away from me."

Mr. Stein beamed and looked at Judd. "I told you our God would provide."

Judd shook his head. He couldn't believe it.

Mr. Stein took the tickets. His eyes filled with tears. "How can we ever thank you?"

"Thank God," Mr. Isaacs said. "He is the one who brought you to me, and he is the one who will lead you to the people who need to hear your message."

"Amen," Mr. Stein said.

SIX

Lenore and Tolan

CONRAD and Mark searched the woods for Janie. When Phoenix lost her trail, they headed toward town on the motorcycle.

Conrad knew it was dangerous anytime the kids got near other people. If the authorities knew the kids lived alone in the country, the GC social services would be after them. The fact that most of the kids believed the message of Tsion Ben-Judah and that they housed a wanted Morale Monitor and an escaped prisoner made Conrad feel queasy.

Mark stopped as they neared the town. Something in the road caught Conrad's eye. "That's a person!"

Mark hid the cycle in some brush. "They must have been trying to find firewood or food during the freeze."

Conrad shook his head. The sight and

smell of the body in the road was awful. He counted five people and several animals alongside the road as they walked into town.

Conrad gave Janie's description to a mechanic at a gas station. The man shook his head but said he'd watch for her.

Conrad turned a corner onto the main street and saw Janie a block away, talking with a woman. Mark pulled him back quickly. A GC squad car passed on another street.

"We have to get to her before they do," Mark said.

Judd's plane left Israel Monday evening. He sat by a window and didn't notice any other believers on the flight. Mr. Stein sat in the middle and talked with an African man. When he brought up the subject of God, the man said he wasn't interested.

The plane landed after midnight in Bamako, Mali. Judd and Mr. Stein passed through the GC checkpoint and wandered into the terminal. Many people had used the airport for shelter during the cold. Clothes and personal belongings sat in piles in hallways.

"What now?" Judd said, feeling a little helpless.

Mr. Stein turned, put a hand on Judd's shoulder, and closed his eyes. "Father, you have led us this far and we thank you. Now we ask you to direct us to the people you want us to reach. We pray in Jesus' name and for his glory. Amen."

Judd looked around. People were staring at them. They moved to the baggage carousel.

"We will wait here," Mr. Stein said.

Judd stretched out on the floor. He was tired and hungry. *I wonder where we'll be this time tomorrow?*

Conrad raced to Janie and pulled her into a nearby alley. Mark kept watch for the GC. The woman with Janie stood near the street, crying. She was holding something under a blanket.

"What's the big idea?" Janie said.

"I can't believe you'd be this stupid!" Mark said.

"I had to get out for a little while," Janie said. "I needed a smoke like you wouldn't believe."

"You didn't see the GC?" Conrad said.

"They're here?" Janie said.

"A squad car just passed a block away

before we got here," Conrad said. "Come back to the school."

"I can't leave her," Janie said, pointing toward the woman. The woman was pale and had long, stringy hair. Her ragged clothes hung on her, and the quilt she carried was filled with holes.

"Lenore," Janie said, "these are two of my friends I was telling you about."

"What?" Mark said. "You told her—"

"She needs a place to stay," Janie said.

"Are you nuts?" Mark said.

"I told her how nice you guys were," Janie said. "Other than the religious stuff, it's okay. Plus there's plenty of food."

"I don't believe this," Mark said.

The woman, sobbing still, put a hand on Mark's arm. "Please, let me come with you. We have nothing. My husband went to find food last week. . . ." Her voice trailed, and she put a hand to her face and wept.

"She found his body this morning," Janie whispered.

"What do you mean, *we?*" Mark said. "Is there somebody else with you?"

Conrad put a hand on Mark's arm and pointed to the edge of the quilt. Sticking out was a tiny, still hand.

"That's her baby," Janie said.

Conrad gasped. "Is it . . . is it dead?"

Lenore pulled the quilt back, showing the baby's face. It was a boy, his tiny hand holding tight to a button on his mother's shirt. Conrad moved closer and noticed the child's chest rising and falling.

Conrad sighed. "I thought he was dead."

"This is Tolan," Lenore said weakly. "He's all I have left."

"I'll help her," Mark said. "There must be some kind of shelter around here. You and Conrad get to the motorcycle."

Janie shook her head. "I'm not leaving her. I'm supposed to do unto others and all that, right? I mean, what if I don't help this lady and her baby dies? You think God would let me into heaven with that on my conscience?"

"It doesn't work that way," Conrad said. "God doesn't let you in because of the good things you do—"

"I don't care what you say," Janie said, "I'm not leaving her."

A car approached. Mark pulled the group behind a huge Dumpster. A GC squad car drove by slowly. When it was gone, Lenore turned to them and whispered, "I won't be a bother. I promise to work for any food we eat. The place this girl told me about sounds wonderful. Please."

Mark pulled Conrad aside. "I don't think we have a choice."

"If we take her, we've opened ourselves up again."

"We have to chance it," Mark said. "If the GC pick Lenore up, she might say something about us. Or she could try and follow us. We can't leave her and the baby alone."

Conrad nodded. "Maybe Zeke can take her to a shelter on his next run through here."

Conrad went ahead of the group, watching for any sign of the GC squad car. When it was safe he motioned to the others. When they found the motorcycle, Lenore and the baby rode with Mark while Janie and Conrad walked.

"Our spiritual guide back at the prison said we're all God's children," Janie said. "Anything we do to another child of God will be repaid in the next life. If we don't do good, we come back as an ant or a snail."

Conrad scratched his head. "God did make all of us, but we aren't all his children."

"You don't think I'm God's child?" Janie said.

"God created you and loved you enough to die for you, but until you receive—"

"I can't believe you don't think I'm a child of God," Janie said. "And that woman and her baby aren't either? No wonder they call you people narrow-minded."

"What you believe is that we're all a part of God and that God rewards and punishes people simply by what they do."

"Yeah, so?"

"God's not like that. He wants to be our friend, but we sinned, and that separates us from God."

Janie interrupted Conrad several times before he gave up. The girl simply wouldn't listen to the truth.

Judd awoke early Tuesday morning with a pain in his neck. He was sore after sleeping against the wall all night. Mr. Stein sat beside him.

"I brought you a donut and some coffee. You like cream and sugar?"

Judd nodded and rubbed his eyes. The donut was stale and the coffee watery, but they still tasted good. He stretched and leaned back against the cold wall. The airport was quiet. A few baggage workers and flight crews walked the halls. Passengers waited for flights in the terminal. A businessman lugged a suit-case up a flight of stairs.

"So what's up?" Judd said.

Mr. Stein smiled. "The sun, for one. And we are both well. We can be thankful for that." Mr. Stein leaned against the wall and cradled his cup of coffee. "If you could have known me before, Judd, you would see what a miracle this is. I am the least likely candidate to be a messenger of God, and yet, here I am."

"But what are we supposed to do?" Judd said.

Mr. Stein closed his eyes. "The psalmist says, 'Wait patiently for the Lord. Be brave and courageous. Yes, wait patiently for the Lord.'

"I think that is the most difficult task we have as followers. Believe. Wait. Let God work in his own time. It must have been very difficult for my daughter to know the truth and still have to wait for me to understand it and believe it."

Judd thought of Chaya and how much she had prayed for her father. "I wish your daughter were here now."

Mr. Stein nodded. "She would be thrilled to see how God has changed my life. Just that I have memorized Scripture would make her laugh with glee."

Mr. Stein said he had read Scripture throughout the night and kept coming back to another passage in the Psalms: "'You will keep on guiding me with your counsel, leading me to a glorious destiny.' And at the end of the psalm he says, 'I will tell everyone about the wonderful things you do.' That is what I want to do more than anything, Judd. Tell people of the wonderful things God can do."

Judd sipped the coffee. He noticed a man in uniform near the baggage carousel watching them. "We have company."

Mr. Stein stood. When the man came closer, Judd saw that he was a pilot and had the mark of the believer.

Mr. Stein shook hands. "Good day to you, my brother."

"Welcome to Mali," the man said. "I am Immen. Did you fly from Jerusalem?"

"Yes," Mr. Stein said, "how did you know?"

"Come with me," Immen said.

"Why?" Judd said.

"God has a job for you," Immen said, "and he has sent me to take you to it."

Vicki was cranky the rest of the day. She barked at Charlie for messing up the food pantry. Mark and Conrad weren't back when it got dark, and she wondered if something was wrong. If they hadn't found Janie in the surrounding woods, they may have gone toward town. That meant possible contact with the GC.

She found an E-mail from Judd and shared it with the rest of the group during dinner. He was off with Mr. Stein to some unknown country. Judd wrote that he didn't know when he and Lionel would be back in the States and asked the kids to pray for Sam, a new friend, and for a "situation" he didn't go into.

"What do you think the other thing is?" Shelly said later as she and Vicki did the dishes.

"Knowing Judd, it's probably something dangerous," Vicki said.

Shelly smiled and looked down at the water.

"What?" Vicki said.

"You and Judd," Shelly said. "I can tell how you feel about him."

Vicki rolled her eyes. "Stop."

Shelly giggled, then put a hand on Vicki's shoulder. "Do you realize how long it's been since any of us has laughed?"

"Just don't make fun of me to get your kicks," Vicki said. "I don't have a thing for Judd."

"Sure," Shelly said.

Outside, a motorcycle revved. Vicki dropped the dishcloth and rushed out. She stared as Mark and an unfamiliar lady stepped off. When the motor died, she heard a baby cry.

Vicki didn't ask questions. Instead, she told Shelly to fix up a room downstairs. Darrion made dinner for their guest. Vicki told Charlie to come up with a crib.

"It's okay," the woman said, "he can sleep with me."

"I'll try anyway," Charlie said.

"Please," the woman said, "don't go to any trouble. I'm just glad to have a place to stay tonight."

"Do you have family?" Vicki said.

The woman began to explain but couldn't continue. She clutched the baby and sobbed.

"It's okay," Vicki said. "We'll get you something to eat and you can rest."

Mark explained what had happened in town. "We're ahead of Janie and Conrad by a few minutes."

Vicki nodded. "We have to figure out what to do with Janie."

SEVEN

Into the Window

JUDD and Mr. Stein followed the pilot through a security door and down a flight of stairs. As they walked onto the runway Judd said, "Where are you taking us?"

Immen stopped. "Are you not the two God has called?"

"We are," Mr. Stein said.

"Good, follow me."

The plane was small. Judd and Mr. Stein had very little room. When they were buckled the pilot quickly went through the preflight procedure and was cleared by the tower.

The plane shook on takeoff, and Judd held on until his knuckles turned white. As they gained altitude, Immen put the plane on autopilot.

"I fly with one of the smaller airlines," Immen said. "I use this to travel home when the roads are impassable."

"How did you know we would be at the airport?" Mr. Stein said.

Immen smiled. "First, you must tell me why it is so urgent that you travel into such a dangerous area."

Mr. Stein shrugged. "We don't know where we're going, my brother. Or what we'll do when we get there. But God has called us." Mr. Stein told Immen about his dream and what he had seen.

Immen shook his head. "God is amazing. I had a dream as well last night. It was during a long flight. My first officer said I was talking in my sleep, but since he's not a believer, I didn't dare tell him what I saw."

"What was the dream?" Judd said.

"I was walking through a remote area, and I came over a sand dune and saw hundreds and thousands of people. I have seen them before from the airplane. They are nomads; they move about the country with their flocks and herds.

"In the dream, these people tried to speak with me. They looked frightened and excited. I was frustrated because I couldn't talk with them or understand them."

"What happened then?" Mr. Stein said.

"I was at the airport. I saw an older man with a beard and a younger man. 'Find them,' a voice said to me.

"I awoke from my dream sweating. It seemed so real."

"We are glad you followed instructions," Mr. Stein said.

The pilot followed a river through the parched land. Judd wondered how the freezing temperatures had affected the desert. A few hours later they landed on a private airstrip, where a friend of Immen's waited. The man greeted Judd and Mr. Stein. He spoke in an African language to Immen, then opened the doors to his home.

"We'll rest here a few hours until sunset," Immen said.

Judd fell into bed and was asleep immediately. When he awoke, Immen's friend had prepared a meal. When they were finished, the man led them outside to his Land Rover.

"Take," the man said.

Mr. Stein hugged the man, and they were off. As they made their way across the rough roads and places where there were no roads, Immen explained. "Many people died from the effects of the cold. My friend told me where he thinks the tribe is staying."

"Do you know their dialect?" Judd said.

"A few words," Immen said. "No one knows their language completely. They have kept to themselves. A few years ago I heard that some of them left the tribe. A few even became Christians. But most remain isolated."

"How did you become a believer?" Judd said.

Immen smiled. "By listening to and reading Tsion Ben-Judah."

Immen drove the Land Rover into the night. Sometime after midnight, they bounced along a dry creek bed, then rose straight up over a sand dune. Immen stopped and pointed. "Down there."

Judd gasped. In the moonlight Judd saw hundreds of campfires. Tents filled the valley, and thousands of dark-skinned people lay sleeping. Goats and camels were tied up at the edge of the camp.

Someone blew a horn, and people shouted and rushed out of their tents. They ran to the center of the village, then headed toward the vehicle. Some carried long, pointed sticks and waved them over their heads.

Judd panicked. "Are we in trouble?"

Immen gunned the engine and raced toward the people. "Not if this is where God wants you to be."

Vicki finally got the woman and baby settled in a room. The baby slept peacefully on a crudely constructed crib Charlie had made from pieces of wood and a few blankets.

As Vicki went for another blanket, Conrad returned with Janie. "I didn't do anything wrong," Janie said when she walked into the kitchen.

Vicki pulled her into the pantry and told her to keep quiet. Vicki shook from anger but tried to control herself. "I can't believe you'd do this to us!"

"This isn't about you," Janie said. "I needed to get away—what's so bad about that?"

Vicki shook her head. "You don't get it, do you?"

"I know the GC could have picked me up, but I wouldn't rat you guys out."

"You have no idea what they can do to you."

Janie stared at Vicki. "Yes I do, but I don't expect you to care about it." She opened the pantry door and slammed it behind her. Vicki sighed and walked into the kitchen.

"I tried to talk with her on the way back. She wouldn't listen," Conrad said.

"I shouldn't have yelled at her like that, but it's so frustrating!"

Vicki took the woman another blanket and a pillow. "My name is Lenore Barker," the woman said quietly. She looked at the sleeping child. "This is Tolan."

Vicki introduced herself and asked if the woman needed anything else.

"No, and I told those two boys that I'm willing to work for any food that I eat."

Vicki smiled. "You'll be safe here tonight."

"Just tonight?" Lenore said. "My husband is gone now and . . ."

Lenore put a hand to her mouth and wept. Vicki patted her shoulder and waited.

"We ran out of food," Lenore said. "We'd burned everything in the house we could to keep warm. Finally, Tim had to go out and try to find some food, or we were going to starve.

"This morning I found him lying in the street a few blocks from our house." Lenore bowed her head and whispered, "He had a loaf of bread and some meat he had found somewhere. He died trying to save our lives."

Vicki shook her head. "I'm so sorry."

"That girl, Janie. She saved my life. I don't know what I would have done if she hadn't come along."

"Somebody would have taken you in," Vicki said.

Lenore shook her head. "When I saw my

husband in the street, I thought about killing myself and my baby. Janie talked me out of it. She said she knew some people who really cared and could help."

"Janie said that?"

"Yeah. She said you were a little weird about reading the Bible but that she was sure you'd give me a place to stay."

Vicki looked at the floor. "She was right. You can stay here as long as you'd like."

Judd watched people swarm around the Land Rover. They shouted and chanted, some with spears held high. They wore loose clothing and many had a cloth around their faces. Their tents were made of camel skin.

"What do we do?" Judd said.

"We will speak to them," Mr. Stein said.

Immen grabbed his arm. "I'm telling you, I only know a few words."

Mr. Stein nodded. "Can you make out anything they're saying?"

Immen listened. "It's something about God. He brings something . . . I'm sorry, I can't make it out."

"He has brought us this far," Mr. Stein said. "He will show us."

The people stood back as the three got out;

then the crowd rushed them and took them to their tents. Judd almost fell and feared being trampled, but they made it safely to the middle of the camp and into the tent of what Judd thought was the leader of the group.

Mr. Stein, Immen, and Judd were forced to sit before a small table. The leader stared at them, then whipped a cloth away, revealing several plates of food. Flies were all over the meat. Judd was handed something warm to drink. He took a sip and nearly gagged.

Immen sat forward and spoke to the leader. The leader replied and Immen asked a question. The leader answered for almost a minute.

"I told him you come in peace and in the name of God," Immen said, "and he said something about a movement of their people. For some reason they've been brought together."

The meal lasted until daybreak. Finally Immen turned to Mr. Stein and said, "They are waiting for some kind of message from the Great Spirit who caused the freeze."

Mr. Stein whispered, "Have them come outside and gather round the Land Rover."

Mr. Stein led Judd through the sea of people. Some were teenagers. They followed him, touching his clothes and chanting something.

When they reached the car, Mr. Stein put a hand on Judd's shoulder. "Please pray as you have never prayed before."

"Immen can't translate," Judd said.

"God will have to provide some other way then."

A few minutes later the leader of the people approached the vehicle. He blew into an animal horn. The people crowded close. Judd figured there must be at least five thousand people.

The leader raised his voice and shouted something. Mr. Stein looked at Immen. "He has introduced you as someone who knows God," Immen said. "I will do my best to translate."

Mr. Stein raised his voice. "Hear the word of the Lord, the maker of the universe, the creator of every living thing."

Before Immen could speak, the people fell to the ground. Even the leader of the group was on his knees.

"Why are you speaking in my language?" Immen said.

"I'm speaking English," Mr. Stein said.

As the people whimpered on the ground, Judd understood. "We're all hearing in our own language. It's just like the witnesses, Eli and Moishe. Tell them something else."

Mr. Stein seemed overwhelmed at the thought that these people were hearing their language supernaturally. He composed himself and said, "Please, stand."

Immediately the entire group stood as one. Judd shook his head. Mr. Stein had been right again. God had worked a miracle to get them there and another after they had arrived.

"There is one God and Creator," Mr. Stein continued, "and he has sent me to tell you he loves you."

As Mr. Stein talked, people looked at each other in amazement. Mr. Stein explained that Jesus, the Son of God, had died as a sacrifice for the bad things people had done. If anyone would come to Jesus and ask forgiveness, God would come into that person's life.

Mr. Stein held up his Bible. The people inched forward, trying to get a look at it. Mr. Stein quoted several verses from Romans that showed that everyone had sinned and that the payment for sin was death and separation from God forever. The people gasped.

"But," Mr. Stein said, "the gift of God is eternal life through Jesus. You will live forever with God if you ask him to forgive you and become your leader."

Many wept when they heard what a terrible death Jesus had died. The leader of the people stepped forward, tears streaming down his cheeks. Mr. Stein led the people in a prayer. Judd couldn't understand anything anyone said except Mr. Stein.

When Mr. Stein finished, the leader of the group climbed onto the Land Rover and hugged him. The people clucked their tongues and cheered. The leader called for quiet and asked a question.

Mr. Stein looked at Immen. "I think," Immen said after a moment, "he said something about their enemy."

"What enemy?" Mr. Stein said.

"There have been many tribal wars throughout the years," Immen said. "People have been killed over a few missing animals. I believe he wants you to give the message to them."

Mr. Stein smiled. "It is proof that they understood my words. We will go wherever God leads us."

EIGHT

The Shooting Star

VICKI called an emergency meeting Wednesday morning. The schoolhouse now housed four unbelievers and an infant.

"This is getting crazy," Mark said. "I thought this place was for training."

"We've asked God to show us what to do, and it seems like he keeps bringing people without the mark," Vicki said. "Maybe that's the kind of training we need."

"More outsiders, more trouble," Mark said.

Shelly sighed. "What about this Carl guy you're supposed to see? You going to bring him back if he's not one of us?"

Mark looked out the window. The sun was coming up and cast an orange glow around the room. "Carl is different. I have to know what happened to John."

The kids were quiet. Darrion leafed

through her Bible and cleared her throat. "I've been reading the book of James. One of the verses says, 'Pure and lasting religion in the sight of God our Father means that we must care for orphans and widows in their troubles, and refuse to let the world corrupt us.' I think all four of our guests qualify."

Vicki nodded and the others agreed. They would care for anyone God brought their way.

While Mark searched the Web, Vicki went to Janie's room. She knew she hadn't treated the girl well the night before. Even if Janie had put them in danger by going off alone, she had cared for Lenore and her baby. Vicki rehearsed what she wanted to say, took a deep breath, and knocked on Janie's door. When there was no answer, she peeked in and found Janie's bed empty.

Not again, Vicki thought.

She searched the house and was about to tell the others when she heard a noise in Lenore's room. The door was slightly open, and Vicki saw Janie holding little Tolan. She was trying to get him to laugh. Lenore lay on the bed behind them, half asleep.

Vicki got Janie's attention. Janie put Tolan beside his mother and walked into the hall.

"You going to yell at me for being in there? I was just trying to help."

"I'm sorry about last night," Vicki said. They walked to Janie's room. "I won't make any excuses. I was wrong to yell at you."

Janie sat on her bed. "And I was wrong to go off like that without talking to you guys."

Vicki sat beside her. "I've been thinking about something you said last night. I couldn't get to sleep wondering what you meant."

"What?" Janie said.

"I said that you have no idea what the GC can do to you if they want information. You said you did. What did you mean?"

Janie put a hand on her elbow and pulled her arm tightly to her chest. "I don't want to talk about it."

Vicki leaned closer. "Maybe it would help."

Tears came to Janie's eyes. "The first place they sent me was awful. I was thrown in with criminals. I thought the detention center was bad, but this was ten times worse.

"I got mixed up with the wrong people. They were bringing drugs into the place. The GC nabbed me and wanted to know who was selling. I wouldn't tell. I knew what would happen as soon as I got back."

Janie pulled up her shirt and turned so Vicki could see. "They stuck this electric thing in my back to get me to talk. The mark's still there."

Vicki shook her head.

"So I know what the GC can do, and I'll say it again. I wouldn't rat on you guys."

Someone shouted in the study room. Vicki excused herself and found Mark typing an answer to an E-mail.

"Carl's going to be dropped off near Kankakee day after tomorrow," Mark said. "I'm going to meet him there."

Conrad looked over Mark's shoulder. "It might be a trap. You know the GC are going to be all over the place."

"We've been through this before," Mark said. "I'm going to hear him out."

Mark searched for the best route to Kankakee, due south of Chicago. Conrad pulled up the latest news, and the others gathered around.

The top story highlighted a shiny object in the sky. At first, stargazers considered it a shooting star. It had first been seen during nighttime hours in Asia. But this star didn't streak across the sky or circle the earth.

A scientist from a leading university said, "Due to the speed of light and the distance from the earth of even the nearest stars, events such as this actually occurred years before and are just being seen now."

But the man had to retract that statement a few hours later. Both amateur and professional astronomers agreed this was no ordinary star and certainly not an event that had happened years before. Though the experts couldn't identify it, they agreed it was falling directly toward Earth. It seemed to emit its own light, as well as reflect light from stars and the sun, depending on the time of day.

The head of the Global Community Aeronautics and Space Administration, GCASA, said it posed very little threat. "It has every chance of burning up as it hits our atmosphere. But even if it remains intact, it will probably land harmlessly in water. If it doesn't vaporize, it will no doubt break apart once it hits the earth."

Vicki watched the coverage with interest. She flipped open her Bible, then asked if she could use the computer. She scrolled through the text of Tsion Ben-Judah's message, looking for a clue.

"What do you make of this?" Conrad said.

Vicki whirled around. "Get downstairs. We don't have much time."

Early Wednesday morning Judd and Mr. Stein arrived at the camp of the enemy tribe.

They had driven to a river and floated in a small boat with the leader and a few others who came with them.

After docking, they hiked to the camp. Several times they heard weird birdcalls. "Those are the scouts sending signals," Immen said. "They will be waiting for us."

"Are you sure about this?" Judd said to Mr. Stein.

"God has not called us to be careful. He has called us to give the message."

A group from the enemy tribe met Judd and the others at the edge of the camp. Judd noticed freshly dug graves nearby and wondered if these people had died from the freeze.

"I know even less of this language," Immen said.

A fierce-looking man from the tribe yelled at them. The others nodded and spoke in agreement. Judd closed his eyes, sure that they would soon be surrounded and killed. But the next voice Judd heard was Mr. Stein's.

"We come on behalf of the Prince of Peace," Mr. Stein said.

Judd could tell the men were amazed that someone was speaking their own language. A crowd from the village gathered. Before long, hundreds were listening to the gospel message. When he finished, Mr. Stein invited the tribe to pray with him.

People knelt and lifted their eyes toward heaven. Many wept. The villagers repeated Mr. Stein's words, though Judd heard what sounded to him like gibberish. When he was finished, Mr. Stein invited the leader of the first tribe to greet the enemy tribe leader. He pointed out the mark of the true believer on their foreheads, and they were both amazed. Two men who had been sworn enemies only minutes before hugged and smiled. Then they hugged Mr. Stein.

"You are to take this message of love and forgiveness to all who need to hear it," Mr. Stein said.

Lionel kept feeding Sam information and Scripture. Like other new believers he had known, Sam was like a sponge. He couldn't get enough teaching about Jesus and the Bible. Though Sam talked about his father often, Lionel was able to keep him from going to see the man.

"I think you'll be able to see him again," Lionel said, "but it's too early right now."

Nada met secretly with Lionel. They talked about the falling object from space and what it might mean. Their conversation finally turned to Judd.

"I am worried that he won't speak with me," Nada said, "that he'll be too concerned about my father."

"Judd respects your dad, and he's grateful for what he's done for us," Lionel said. "But I won't let him leave here without having a talk with you."

"I want more than a talk," Nada said. "I want to go to your country. I feel so trapped here. I want to be a part of the Young Tribulation Force."

Lionel smiled. "You don't have to go back to the States to be part of our group. As a matter of fact, you might wind up being more help to us staying here. If it weren't for you, we probably wouldn't have gotten Sam out of his dad's house."

Nada's father knocked on the door. She put a finger to her lips and stood behind it. The door opened, and Jamal handed the phone to Lionel. "Please speak quickly," Jamal said, "I am waiting for an important call."

Lionel took the phone. It was Judd.

"You won't believe what's happened," Judd said. He explained the adventure he and Mr. Stein had been through.

"Where are you now?" Lionel said.

"We're spending a couple more days here so Mr. Stein can train the new evangelists," Judd said. "The guy who flew us here is bringing us back to Bamako on Sunday. We're hoping to get a flight into Israel from there. Can you meet us at the airport?"

"I'll be there," Lionel said.

"Good. I want us to fly to the States from there. We have to get back to the others."

"Sounds great," Lionel said, "but what about money?"

"God is working," Judd said. "If he wants us to get home, we'll get there."

When Lionel hung up, he went to the computer.

"What are you doing?" Nada said.

"Maybe there's some way the others can help us get back," Lionel said.

Vicki helped Mark load his backpack onto the motorcycle. He said it would take him a day to get to Kankakee, and he wanted to get there early to scope things out before he met with Carl. "Sorry I can't help with downstairs," he said.

"We'll manage," Vicki said. "We've got the lower room almost sealed off."

"Are you sure about what you're doing down there?" Mark said.

"No," Vicki said, "but if I'm right, all this work will pay off."

Mark said good-bye to everyone and rode off. Shelly called the others inside. She had just gotten Lionel's E-mail.

Conrad slammed some tools down and said, "That's it. I'm going to get that safe open if it's the last thing I do."

Vicki met with Lenore briefly to make sure she had what she needed. "What are you doing downstairs?" Lenore said.

"We're preparing," Vicki said. "I don't want to scare you, but I think this judgment will be even worse than the others."

Lenore frowned. "Janie said you people were kind of strange when it came to religion."

"I'd like to explain what we believe if you'll let me," Vicki said.

Tolan stirred in his crib and started crying. "I need to feed him right now. Maybe later."

Vicki went back to the study room, where the kids watched the latest on the falling object. It had landed without doing any damage. The head of GCASA was back at a news conference to explain.

"The point of impact is in a remote area near the border of Syria and Iraq," the man said. "We have not been able to locate the object in our aerial studies. It appears to have slipped past the earth's surface into a deep crevice."

A reporter shot up a hand. "Sir, can't you get teams in there to find it and study it?"

"It's impossible to get a vehicle in that area or even get a team in there on foot. Our main concern is what might have been done to the earth's crust. We haven't been able to detect a problem at this point, but we want to make sure."

Suddenly Vicki and the others felt a tremor. The schoolhouse shook slightly, and then all was calm. "Did you feel that?" Lenore said as she ran in with her baby. "It's not another earthquake, is it?"

The head of GCASA was handed a piece of paper from an aide. "I've just received this report and won't be able to answer any questions. It says there's been an eruption near the place where the object fell. We have data from different countries coming in that say their sensors went off the scale a few moments ago. Our pilots monitoring the area were blown off course and forced to escape the area."

The GCASA leader quickly exited the news conference with reporters screaming questions. A few minutes later, pictures from a news flight showed the beginning of a mushroom cloud a thousand times bigger than anything seen in history.

"We are now told," a news anchor reported, "that this object has somehow triggered volcano-like activity deep beneath the surface of the earth's crust."

Judd and Mr. Stein were in the Land Rover when the thick, black cloud rolled across the desert. There was no wind to speak of, but the cloud moved rapidly, blotting out the sun. The thick cloud almost seemed solid as it rolled over the landscape. As it traveled quickly above them, Judd could tell this wasn't a smoky cloud that thinned as it moved. It was dense and as black as the base of a gasoline fire. From the radio Judd learned that scientists feared the source of the smoke was a huge fire that would eventually rise and shoot flames miles into the air.

"We must hurry if we hope to get back to Israel by Sunday," Mr. Stein said.

NINE

Cracking the Safe

MARK arrived in Kankakee, Illinois, Wednesday night. It had been a grueling ride. He found a cheap hotel by the interstate and fell asleep.

The next morning, he drove to the airport but saw no Global Community officers. An older man at the information desk told him the Global Community had a temporary post set up outside the terminal. The man had no idea when Carl's flight might arrive.

Mark kept his distance from the GC. Though Nicolae Carpathia said everyone could travel as they pleased, Mark knew he had to be careful. He saw one officer walk outside to smoke near a chain-link fence. Mark approached him and said hello. The man ignored him. His nameplate said "Kolak."

"I'm wondering about the transport flight that's supposed to be here today," Mark said.

"Nobody's supposed to know about those flights," the officer said.

"I don't know what's on them," Mark said quickly. "I've got a friend coming in from South Carolina who said he'd be here today. I told him I'd pick him up."

Kolak blew smoke in Mark's face and laughed. "Heard there was a flight from down south that got cancelled because of the cloud. Might be here Saturday."

"Saturday!?" Mark said.

"Could be Sunday," Kolak said. "What's your friend's name?"

Mark didn't want to give the man too much information, but he also didn't want the guy to get suspicious.

"Carl Meninger," Mark said.

Kolak threw his cigarette to the ground and smashed it with his foot. "You mean one of the guys on the sub?"

"I don't know," Mark said. "What sub?"

"Communications guy on the *Peace-keeper 1*, right?"

"I guess so," Mark said.

"How do you know him?"

"I had a cousin on that ship," Mark said. "Carl wanted to talk to me."

"Come with me," Kolak said. He pointed to the gate in the fence.

Mark hesitated.

"Well, come on, I want to make sure you and your buddy get hooked up."

Mark followed the man inside the fence to a small building. Inside were three GC officers standing by television monitors. Nicolae Carpathia smiled at the camera.

"I bid all workers of the Global Community greetings. Your hard work and efforts to bring peace and harmony to people around the globe do not go unnoticed."

Carpathia held a piece of paper in his hand. "As you know, a few days ago I gave approval for all those who follow religions other than Enigma Babylon One World Faith to travel about freely. I also cleared them of any wrongdoing in Israel.

"At the request of people I trust, I am today issuing an order that gives Peter the Second, Supreme Pontiff of Enigma Babylon One World Faith, the authority to handle this situation. Since it is a religious issue that separates the followers of Dr. Ben-Judah from the One World Faith, I am giving him full power to handle this in whatever way he chooses.

"After Pontiff Mathews looks the matter over, I assume he will make a statement to the media. Until then, be alert for any terrorist acts these followers may attempt. Thank you for your service."

The men clapped. One said, "I hope they get those jerks and put them in jail."

The head officer turned and looked at Mark. "How long's he been here?"

Kolak stepped forward. "This kid says he's here to meet with Meninger, one of the survivors from the *Peacekeeper 1.*"

The officer nodded. "All right. Give us your number and we'll let you know when he's supposed to get here."

Mark nodded and wrote the number of the hotel on a scrap of paper. As he walked out, he wondered if he had just done something that would come back to haunt him.

Vicki took some food to Lenore. Tolan had a runny nose and a cough and the woman seemed upset. Vicki looked for some infant medicine but couldn't find any.

She heard a commotion in the study room. When she arrived, everyone was crowded around Conrad. "I did it!" Conrad said when he saw Vicki. "I got it open, and you're not going to believe what's in here."

Conrad lugged the safe to the computer table. "I took Melinda's advice and worked on the body instead of the lock. There was a little rust in one corner of the bottom. I got a drill bit through—"

"Who cares how you got it open?" Janie said. "Just show us what's inside."

Conrad flipped the safe upside down and put his hand through the small opening. He pulled out a gold coin. "It's full of them. Has to be worth thousands, maybe hundreds of thousands!"

"We have to call Z," Vicki said. "If he gives us the okay, we could sell some of them and get the money to Judd and Lionel."

"Why do we have to call anybody?" Janie said.

"This is Z's property," Conrad said. "We don't do anything until we've cleared it with him."

Vicki dialed the number and explained to Z what had happened.

"That's good work," Z said. "We been lookin' for that box since I was a kid. Never looked in the bell tower."

"We'd like to sell a few of the coins and get the money to Judd and Lionel to get back to the States," Vicki said.

"Might take a while to get a buyer," Z said. "Tell you what I'll do. I'll wire the money to Israel. You find out where to send it and all the details. I'll come pick up the coins on my next run."

"Do you have any infant medicine?" Vicki said. She explained about Lenore and how it seemed God was bringing them more and more nonbelievers to live with them.

Z laughed. "Sounds like he's throwing a few monkey wrenches into your plans."

Vicki sighed. "If this is what God wants us to do, we'll do it."

"I may have some aspirin for the baby," Z said, "but it might take a few days. Call me if things get worse."

Judd awoke in the middle of the night, troubled. The temperatures during the day had risen above a hundred degrees. During the night he tossed and turned inside the Land Rover, trying to figure out what to do. Mr. Stein had said he felt God wanted him to stay and train more people.

In the morning, Judd walked with Mr. Stein. Yet another encampment of people stood before them. Hundreds milled about with what was left of their flocks and herds.

"I can't leave," Mr. Stein said. "I believe God has called me to this."

"I wouldn't ask you to leave," Judd said,

"but I think I should get back to Lionel and Sam."

"I understand," Mr. Stein said, looking at the people. "Isn't this amazing? God has prepared their hearts for his message. It is almost as if I don't need to say anything. They already hunger for God's forgiveness."

Judd looked up at the cloud that didn't end. God was up to something. He was also working in Judd's life. Judd had grown spiritually as he watched Mr. Stein speak to the new believers. He had seen God work in a way Judd would never dream of, and it had changed him.

But Judd also felt a longing to share his experiences with someone. Even with his friends around, he felt lonely. He wanted to share this experience with someone close.

Judd thought of Nada. She was certainly interested in him. But his thoughts turned to Vicki. *Could anything ever work out between us?* he thought.

Mr. Stein handed Judd the rest of his money. "I will see if Immen can get you to the airport in Bamako. You should be able to get a flight to Israel if the planes haven't been grounded."

"What about you?" Judd said.

Mr. Stein smiled. "God is looking out for both of us. He will show us where to go and what to do."

Lionel was excited to hear the news from Vicki that their plane fare could be wired to Israel. Lionel figured it would be safer if the money was wired in Sam's name, so he gave Vicki the information.

"Z says the money should be there Saturday afternoon," Vicki said.

"Is everybody all right back there?" Lionel asked.

"We had a pretty big scare through the freeze, but everybody's pulling together now. Well, almost everybody."

"I think I know who you mean," Lionel said.

"Have you heard from Judd?"

Lionel briefly gave Vicki Judd's report. "I hope we can get back home before the next judgment hits."

Mark waited in his hotel room. Friday came and went with no sign of Carl's plane. Mark watched the TV coverage of the cloud that had enveloped the earth. It looked as dark as night outside, and he wondered how any plane could get through the inky blackness.

Lionel told Nada about the money they were expecting. She closed her eyes and frowned. "Are all three of you leaving?" she said.

"We hope to take Sam with us, if he wants to go," Lionel said.

As the two talked, Jamal walked in. "Father, I'm going with Lionel to retrieve a wire."

Jamal looked at Lionel. "She goes nowhere with you."

Lionel held up both hands. "I didn't ask her, sir."

Jamal ordered Nada to her room and turned to Lionel. "This is the final warning. If you talk to my daughter again, I will ask you to leave."

"Understood," Lionel said. "Can we borrow your car to pick up—"

Jamal shook his head. "It's too dangerous now. I can't let you out with my vehicle."

Lionel and Sam left through the back entrance and found a bus that ran close to the bank. Before they reached it, Lionel and Sam split up. Lionel sat in an outdoor café across the street and watched.

As the plane touched down in Bamako, Judd thanked Immen and offered to pay him.

"Do not insult me," Immen said. "Besides, I believe you will need all of that cash to get back to Israel."

Immen gave Judd the name of another believer he could call on in case he had trouble. Inside the airport Judd discovered that many flights had been cancelled because of the dark cloud. The only airline that offered flights to Israel wouldn't get him there until Monday. Plus, the airfare was more than Mr. Stein had given him.

Judd tried to bargain with the ticket agent, but he wouldn't budge from the listed price.

Great, Judd thought, *what do I do now?*

At the outdoor café, Lionel asked for a glass of water. The waiter scowled and said something in another language. Lionel pointed to a soft drink, and the waiter frowned and took his menu.

Sam entered the bank. Lionel could see him through a row of windows in front. The boy stopped and said something to a security guard, then got in line. *So far so good*, Lionel thought.

As Sam moved forward, Lionel noticed two men in a car scanning the bank with binoculars. As Sam reached the teller the men quickly exited the car and headed for the front door. They didn't wear GC uniforms, but Lionel knew they were probably working with Sam's father.

Lionel stood. He wanted to get Sam's attention, but he couldn't. If Lionel didn't act now, Sam and the money would be gone. He glanced up the street for any other suspicious cars. Nothing.

Lionel crossed the street. Someone behind him shouted. It was the waiter holding a soda. Lionel shrugged and kept moving.

Sam signed something at the teller window and waited for his money. Lionel moved past the two men at the door and reached the security guard. He asked where the men's rest room was, and the man pointed to a hallway.

"There's a couple of suspicious guys out front," Lionel said. "Looks like they're about to jump somebody. Thought you oughta know."

The guard thanked Lionel and spoke into a walkie-talkie.

That ought to keep them busy a few minutes, Lionel thought.

Sam stuffed a wad of cash into a pocket and turned. Lionel called out and motioned for him. Sam looked around nervously, then followed. When they were inside the bathroom, Lionel said, "Give me the money. There are two guys outside waiting for you."

"My dad," Sam said, handing over the money.

Lionel looked for a window but found none. "The security guard may keep them busy for a couple of minutes. Is there a back way out of this place?"

Sam nodded. "An alarm will sound."

"Good," Lionel said. "Stay right here."

TEN

The Voice

As Lionel exited the bathroom door, he saw the two men still outside in a wild conversation with the security guard.

Lionel crept down the carpeted hallway and hit the door, sounding the alarm. He rushed back to the men's room and shoved Sam out of sight.

Keys jangled outside. People ran past. "Okay," Lionel said, "follow me."

Lionel and Sam calmly walked into the lobby. As Lionel suspected, the two men had rushed out the back door. The security guard wasn't in sight.

Lionel and Sam didn't run until they turned the corner. They stayed out of sight until they reached the bus stop.

Judd phoned Immen's friend and explained the situation. The man asked which airline he had chosen and told Judd to wait fifteen minutes, then return to the ticket window. Judd got back in line and a half hour later was talking with the same ticket agent who had turned him down earlier. Judd gave his information and said, "I've made arrangements with a friend."

The ticket agent scowled and tapped his keyboard. The man raised his eyebrows. "It looks like someone has made up the rest of the price of the ticket."

Judd handed the cash to the man and signed a form. "When will that flight leave?"

"They're talking about Sunday evening. Perhaps Monday morning."

Judd shook his head.

"It's the weather phenomenon," the agent said. "If you'd like a refund, I can—"

"No," Judd said, "I'll take it."

Judd took the ticket and went to his gate. He called Lionel, but there was no answer. He found a restaurant that had E-mail access and typed a message to Lionel, then sent one to Vicki and the others back in Illinois.

Mark wished he had taken Judd's laptop with him. Late Sunday evening he watched the GC coverage of the cloud. He clicked to other channels and found psychics and fortune-tellers. Viewers wanted to know the future, and they were willing to take answers, even if the answers were wrong.

Flipping through more channels, Mark landed on a movie and thought of his cousin John. They used to love watching action flicks together. This one had some bad language, but he overlooked it because he was so interested in the plot. But things on the screen got worse. He reached for the remote and turned off the television.

Mark shook his head. Before he had become a believer in Christ he had watched things he knew were wrong. The images had stayed with him, even after becoming a believer. Now he felt ashamed that he had been drawn in. He unplugged the television and opened his Bible.

The phone rang. It was the guard, Kolak. "Boss wanted me to tell you that transport plane is supposed to get here between 8:00 and 9:00 tomorrow morning."

"Do you know if Carl is on the flight?" Mark said.

"Don't know anything other than that the flight's due in the morning. I'd be here if I were you."

Judd ate an overpriced meal at an airport restaurant. He had saved a few dollars to get him to Israel, but his money supply was down to almost nothing. His flight number was called over the loudspeaker. An airline representative said the flight had again been delayed. They hoped to get off the ground at some point Monday morning.

Judd groaned and settled into a chair in the waiting room. He propped his feet up and watched the television monitors. The continued effects of the worldwide cloud were the top story. Scientists speculated that the falling object had created a volcanic disturbance underground. "We should see this cloud cover dissolve within the next few days," one scientist said.

The news switched to a statement from Peter the Second. The man was wearing his full clerical outfit. "The Global Community may have an agreement with these religious terrorists, the followers of Rabbi Ben-Judah,

but the time has come to enforce the law.
Enigma Babylon One World Faith is the
accepted religion for the whole world. I have
read the rules listed in the Global Community charter, and I believe it is now within
my power to punish offenders.

"So that all may be clear, I consider the
intolerant, one-way-only beliefs as a threat to
true religion. Therefore, Enigma Babylon
must go on the offensive.

"To be an atheist or an agnostic is one
thing. Even they are welcome. But it is illegal
to practice a form of religion that opposes
our mission. Followers of Dr. Tsion Ben-
Judah will suffer."

Judd felt a chill run down his spine. *So
much for being able to live your life in freedom,*
Judd thought.

"As a first step to rid the world of intoler-
ance, it shall be deemed criminal, as of
midnight Tuesday, for anyone to visit the
Web site of the so-called Tribulation Force.
The teachings of this cult's guru are poison to
people of true faith and love, and we will not
tolerate his deadly teachings."

Several people in the airport clapped and
cheered. Judd looked around for someone
with the mark of the believer but saw no one.

"Technology is in place that can monitor

the Internet activity of every citizen,"
Mathews continued, "and those who visit
this site after the deadline shall be subject to
fine and imprisonment."

Mark awoke early Monday morning, checked
out of the hotel, and drove to the airport. He
parked his motorcycle a good distance away
from the GC post. He had seen and heard
very few planes land at the airport and wondered whether the flight might again be cancelled.

Kolak came to the fence and gave Mark a
thumbs-up sign. "Ten more minutes!" he
yelled.

A few minutes later the jet engine
screamed overhead. The plane descended
through the dense cloud with a roar.
Through the noise, Mark heard a voice. He
turned, thinking someone was behind him.
There was no one there.

Monday afternoon in Israel, Lionel and Sam
said good-bye to Jamal and his family. Nada
came out of her room and hugged Lionel.
She began to speak, then looked at her father

and stepped back. Her mother put an arm around her and pulled her close.

"I can't thank you enough for taking us in," Lionel said. "I don't know what we would have done."

Jamal nodded. "If I had come to your country, I'm sure you would have done the same for me."

Jamal drove Lionel and Sam to the airport and dropped them at the terminal. "May God protect you, my friends," Jamal said before he drove off.

Lionel checked the monitors inside and found the right gate. His heart sank when he heard an announcement that said all outgoing flights had just been cancelled. Lionel rushed to Judd's gate and talked with the attendant.

"That flight is already in the air," the attendant said. "It should be here within the hour."

"Why is everything being cancelled?" Lionel said.

"Radar shows that the cloud mass is increasing," the attendant said. "There's a good chance of severe weather ahead."

Lionel sat with Sam in the waiting area. The boy was quiet.

"Want to talk about it?" Lionel said.

Sam looked out the huge windows. "It's my dad. I want to talk with him."

Lionel nodded. "You know if you reach out to him what's going to happen. Those guys at the bank showed you that."

Sam stared out the window.

Announcements were made over the loudspeaker about cancelled flights. People hurried back and forth. Some shouted at attendants.

Lionel closed his eyes and put his head back. He heard a voice that sounded like it was right next to him. He opened his eyes and stared at Sam.

"Did you hear that?" Lionel said.

"Yes," Sam said, "it was perfect Hebrew."

"Hebrew?" Lionel said. "I heard it in English."

Others around them had heard the voice as well. Some women ran screaming into the rest room. A businessman carrying a briefcase fell to the floor and scampered under some seats. A woman at the gate got on the loudspeaker. "Please stay calm!" she shouted.

"What was it?" Sam said.

"The angel," Lionel said. "It's sounding the next judgment."

Judd had fallen asleep on the crowded airplane. The seats were small and the plane seemed ancient. As he dozed, he thought of the trip with Mr. Stein and what he had learned. Once again he ached to share the experience with someone close to him.

He awoke suddenly, thinking another passenger had said something. The man next to him shrieked, unbuckled, and jumped into the aisle. A woman in front of Judd did the same, and the two ran into each other.

"What's happening?" a woman yelled behind Judd.

The plane descended into the thick cloud, and the plane was enveloped in darkness. Those who weren't screaming or crying whimpered in fear.

Judd thought of Mr. Stein and the kids back in Illinois. If he could hear the voice of the angel in an airplane, could everyone on the ground hear it too? Judd sat forward and looked around. He was the only one with the mark of the believer. He was the only one who knew what was about to happen.

Vicki asked the group to come together in the study room early Monday morning. Melinda was walking with only a slight limp now, her foot almost back to normal. Conrad couldn't wait for Z to come so he could show him the gold coins. Thankfully, Tolan's temperature was normal. Janie complained about the meeting but showed up anyway.

Vicki turned on a light and ran through the changes that had been made downstairs. "We've made it as airtight as possible. I don't think it can be any more secure."

"Why'd you guys do all that work?" Janie said. "Doesn't make sense."

Vicki put her hands on her hips. "We did it for you. And for the others here who don't believe what we're telling you is true."

Janie rolled her eyes.

Vicki began the teaching for the day. Tsion Ben-Judah's latest teaching concerned the next judgment. She called up notes on the computer.

"I've told you what Dr. Ben-Judah thinks about the cloud that's covering the earth. Tsion says the things that come from it will not be part of the animal kingdom at all, but actual demons that—"

Vicki stopped when she heard the noise. It sounded from the heavens, reverberated outside, but they could all hear it clearly in the room.

"Woe, woe, woe to the inhabitants of the earth, because of the remaining blasts of the trumpet of the three angels who are about to sound!"

Phoenix barked at the voice of the angel. Charlie's eyes widened. He grabbed the dog in fear.

"What was that?" Melinda said.

Janie shook her head. "You think we'll fall for anything. That came from the computer."

Conrad stared at Janie. "No, it didn't."

"She had it on a timer or something," Janie said. "You guys can't scare us into believing."

"We wouldn't do that," Conrad said.

Vicki held up a hand. "These judgments are going to get worse and worse. The only way to survive is to ask God to forgive you."

Before anyone else could speak, Janie said, "If you're so smart, tell me what's going to happen." She snickered and looked around the room. "Is it going to be a God-sized tornado? Is that cloud going to spew out a bunch of little green men? Sounds like I'm not the only person here who's smoked some weed."

Darrion got in Janie's face. "These are going to be the scariest things you've ever seen in your life. I wouldn't make fun of them if I were you."

"We may not have much time," Vicki said. She and Shelly helped Lenore carry the baby and his crib downstairs. Melinda and Charlie weren't far behind.

Janie stayed in the room. "I'll ride this one out with the religious weirdos!"

ELEVEN

Apollyon

As JUDD's plane descended into the cloud, the captain of the flight spoke on the intercom, first in French, then in English. "Do not be alarmed by the voice you just heard. We believe there was some kind of interference with the plane's sound system."

Judd shook his head. *These people will never believe*, he thought.

The announcement by the pilot seemed to calm people. Those who had gone into the aisle made their way back to their seats. Some laughed nervously, as if they hadn't really been frightened.

The pilot came back on the intercom. "We're descending into the cloud. Don't be alarmed by the darkness as we prepare for landing."

Judd sat in the middle seat and craned his neck to see out the window. "You want to move over here?" the man beside him said. "There's nothing out there but pitch-black."

A flash of lightning lit the cloud. In that split second, Judd looked past the man and saw something swirling, almost like a tornado, inside the cloud. "If you don't mind, I would like to switch seats."

"Suit yourself," the man said.

Judd moved over and peered out the window. A flight attendant instructed everyone to put down their window shades. Judd dutifully followed orders, then lifted it slightly and bent to see outside.

Another flash of lightning revealed an incredible sight. In the swirling blackness, small pieces of the cloud were breaking off. The pieces scattered and flew through the air. At first, Judd thought it was an actual tornado. He had heard how fierce winds could lift pieces of wood and stone into the air thousands of feet. But these bits of debris seemed to have a mind of their own. They flew in all directions.

"Close that now!" the attendant yelled from the aisle.

"Sorry," Judd said. He put the shade all the way down and sat back.

The man in the middle seat snickered. "She really told you." He patted Judd on the shoulder. "Don't worry, we'll be out of the cloud in a few minutes and you can look all you want."

"Flight attendants, prepare for landing," the pilot said over the intercom.

Suddenly, the plane was splattered with small objects. It sounded like hail. The plane dipped and veered to the left, as if trying to avoid something. The pilot came back on the intercom. This time he sounded out of control. "Please do *not* look out the window! We're experiencing some kind of weather phenomenon." Judd heard someone scream in the cockpit. The captain turned off the intercom.

People around Judd began to whimper again. The man in the aisle seat nervously fidgeted with an in-flight magazine. He turned to the man in the middle. "I've been through hail in a plane smaller than this one. This shouldn't be a problem."

From three rows behind Judd came a piercing scream. Then another. Someone had ignored the captain's order and had looked out.

Judd slammed open his window shade.

Mark watched the GC plane land and taxi to the end of the runway. Kolak and two other

officers drove a jeep to pick up the pilots.
Mark saw a younger officer with a backpack
get out. He was tall with dark hair and eyes.
The man jumped out of the jeep before it
stopped and trotted toward the fence. "Are
you Mark?"

Mark nodded. "Carl?"

They shook hands. "Man, that was scary
up there," Carl said, taking off his hat. There
was no mark on his forehead. "We heard a
voice in the plane."

Mark's heart sunk. He couldn't take Carl
back to the schoolhouse. And with the judgment coming, Mark knew he had only a little
time to convince him of the truth.

"The pilots said it might be somebody
jamming the GC radio signals," Carl said. He
grabbed a jacket from his backpack, and
Mark spotted a Bible inside.

"I wish your cousin were here," Carl said.
"Bet he could explain all this."

"Yeah," Mark said, picking up the Bible.
John's name was written on the front.

"He gave me that before he died. I want to
explain what happened. I have some questions, too."

"We have to talk," Mark said.

"Yeah, but I want to get away from here
first."

"We may not have much time," Mark said.

"What do you mean?"

"Carl, I heard the voice down here."

"You had a radio?"

"It didn't come over the radio." Mark stepped closer. "It was an angel announcing—"

"No way," Carl said, "you're trying to scare me."

"The angel sounded a warning to everybody on earth. You'd better listen to it."

"You don't even know what the voice said."

"'Woe, woe, woe, to the inhabitants of the earth . . . ,'" Mark said.

Carl squinted. "How did you know that?"

"God is about to bring a judgment on the people who haven't given their lives to him. Did John talk to you about this?"

"Sort of," Carl said. "He wanted me to pray with him, but I didn't feel right about it."

"What more do you need to know?" Mark said. "All you have to realize is that—"

Carl shook his head and interrupted. "Let's get away from here so I can think clearly. Take me to you guys' hideout and I'll tell you all about it."

Mark blinked. How did Carl know they had a hideout? He pushed the thought from

his mind and led Carl to his motorcycle.
"Hope you don't mind riding on the back."

Carl smiled. "I haven't ridden one of these in a couple of years. It'll be great."

As they pulled out the wind picked up. Dust and sand flew at them from the runway. Mark headed toward the interstate and noticed the cloud changing as they drove. The underside turned from a dark blue to a yellowish brown.

"Something's happening," Carl yelled over the noise of the motorcycle engine.

Mark turned his head to answer, but the sight over Carl's shoulder sent a chill through him. The cloud was falling to the earth. Mark couldn't speak. He knew what was about to happen and he had no way of stopping it.

Lionel took Sam to the corner of the airport waiting area and watched as people scurried about. The minutes just after the angel spoke were chaotic. People screamed and ran for cover, but they didn't know what they were running from. Finally things calmed. People checked on incoming flights. Others who had just discovered that all outbound flights had been cancelled complained and stomped off.

Lionel stood by the window and watched for Judd's plane. As it descended from the cloud, it veered to the right, then angled downward toward the runway.

"Look," Sam said, "the cloud is changing."

Sam was right. The bottom of the cloud swirled, like a beehive suspended in midair. Instead of dark blue, the cloud had taken on a yellowish color. As the plane fell from the sky, the cloud seemed to follow it.

"What's that noise?" Sam said.

It began as a low humming sound and became louder. Lionel looked up. The cloud was breaking apart. Little pieces fell to earth.

The noise was deafening, like a helicopter, only higher pitched and metallic.

"Sounds like a gigantic lawn mower," Sam said, covering his ears. Others in the airport did the same as the clanging continued. Lionel's body shook from the beating and rattling outside the window. His heart raced.

On the other side of the terminal came a tapping on the windows. People shrieked and scattered, pointing and crying. Lionel glanced out the window and saw creatures fly out of the cloud. They flew fast and swarmed like bees.

A mix of brown, black, and yellow, the locusts were hideous. They looked like tiny horses about six inches long with scorpion-like tails. Lionel was close enough to the window to look into their eyes. They were on the attack. The creatures seemed to look past Lionel and Sam to the others in the terminal. The earthquake and meteors had been devastating to live through. But these beings were the most horrible things he had ever seen.

Lionel noticed a door that led to the gate. Someone had left it open. He sprinted across the waiting area and slammed it shut. Then came the anguished scream of a worker just outside the door. The man was covered with the creatures and was trying to get inside.

Judd had read Tsion Ben-Judah's description of the demon locusts, but it had not prepared him for his first sight of them. *Ugly* was too nice a word. Just a glimpse at one turned Judd's stomach. The man next to him fainted. People all around Judd screamed for help. Judd pulled down the window shade.

Tsion had taught that these creatures wouldn't harm plants like normal locusts did. Instead, they would attack those who did not have the seal of God on their foreheads. If that was true, Judd was the only one on the plane who wasn't a target.

Another frightening observation of Rabbi Ben-Judah was that the people who were stung would be in so much pain that they would want to die, but God would not allow them to. Tsion said these beasts were not part of the animal kingdom at all. Instead, they were actual demons taking the form of living organisms. Even though the plane was traveling at a high speed, the demon locusts swarmed over it.

Screaming continued throughout the cabin as an explosion rocked the plane. The pilot came back on the intercom, panic in his voice. "We've just lost our right engine! We have to make an emergency landing. Everyone assume the crash position."

Some of those things must have gotten sucked inside, Judd thought. He opened the window shade again. A huge ball of fire engulfed the engine. White liquid poured into the hole, putting out the fire, but they were falling fast. An emergency crew drove wildly toward the runway. Judd shook his head. *They'll get stung before they can ever help us.*

Somehow the pilot managed to get the plane safely on the ground. People clapped nervously, but as soon as they rolled to a stop, the shrieking and wailing began again. The metallic sound of the locusts roared outside.

The creatures surrounded the plane and hovered, beating their wings and driving their heads into the windows. The sound of scratching at the roof of the plane made passengers cower in their seats.

Judd opened the shade and put his face close to the window. One of the beasts rammed its head into the glass and was stunned. It shook and looked directly at Judd. Judd was sickened by what he saw. The face of the locust looked like a man's. The eyes were hollow and piercing. The mouth dripped saliva from teeth that were long and pointed, like a lion's. Another disgusting feature was the demon's long, flowing hair. It spilled out from under what looked like a gold crown.

The creature flew forward and hovered at the top of the window so it could look past Judd to the other passengers. When it caught a glimpse of the others, the locust bared its teeth and struggled desperately to get inside.

Judd shuddered. No way they could open the door without those things getting inside. Everyone on the plane was trapped.

Mark gunned the motorcycle, but he couldn't outrun the beasts from the sky. They fell from the dark cloud above and scattered. Mark figured he had only seconds to find shelter for Carl.

Mark spotted a car under a bridge and screeched to a stop. "Quick, get inside!"

Carl jumped from the cycle and lifted the door handle. "It's locked!"

"Try the other side!" Mark yelled.

The noise from the approaching creatures grew to a roar. Cars passing above on the bridge crashed into each other at the sight of the oncoming horde. Mark looked up and saw the beasts already on the bridge.

"The back door's open!" Carl yelled.

"Get in and make sure the windows are all up!" Mark shouted.

Carl closed the door just as the locusts descended, skittering on the windshield and banging their heads into the windows. Carl scooted to the other side and reached for the doorknob.

"No!" Mark yelled, "I'm okay. Just stay where you are!"

Mark knew from his study that he wouldn't be stung by the locusts, but his heart raced when he saw them swarm around the car. Their wings clattered, and they hissed at the sight of their victim. Mark wondered if Carl could be stung more than once.

Someone screamed from above, and Mark ran to the edge of the bridge. A man had gotten out of his car, and several of the demon locusts had swarmed around him. "They're biting me!" the man yelled, climbing onto the bridge railing.

Mark yelled at him but it was too late. The man stepped off and plunged to the pavement. Mark knew the fall had to be fatal. He ran to the man's side and was surprised to find a pulse. A huge welt appeared on the man's arm where a locust had stung him. Mark leaned over the man's face and said, "Sir, can you hear me?"

To Mark's surprise, the man rolled over and groaned. "I wanted to kill myself. It hurts so much. I want to die!"

Mark turned back to the abandoned car and felt a chill. Someone or something was chanting. He walked closer to the car and listened as more locusts swarmed near Carl.

"Apollyon!" the beasts shouted. "Apollyon, Apollyon, Apollyon!"

Vicki closed the door to the secret room downstairs and made sure the second door was secure as well. She was glad she could offer shelter to those who wanted safety. She hoped all their work on the rooms would pay off.

Janie was still making fun of the kids upstairs. She believed the voice of the angel was a hoax.

"You'd better get downstairs while you can," Conrad said.

A low rumble shook the windows of the schoolhouse.

"It's too late," Vicki said, coming up the stairs. "They'll be here any minute."

"Who'll be here?" Janie said.

Vicki shook her head. "We tried to warn you, Janie. You wouldn't listen."

Janie went to the window and looked out. "Something's happening. What's that sound?"

"Your worst nightmare," Conrad said.

Something banged into the windows in the front room. Roaring, buzzing, and clanging filled the house.

"Okay, okay," Janie said, "take me downstairs."

"We can't put the others at risk," Vicki said.

"Just open the door and let me go down!" Janie screamed.

The demon locusts angrily converged on the schoolhouse. Though Conrad and Darrion had checked all the windows, somehow a few locusts managed to get inside.

"The kitchen pantry!" Vicki yelled.

Janie ran for the back of the house, but a locust roared down the stairs and attacked. Janie flailed at the creature and knocked it to the wooden floor, but another flew after her. Conrad picked up a piece of firewood and knocked the beast against a wall. It lay there, stunned.

Janie rushed into the pantry and grabbed the door. Just as she closed it, another locust darted inside.

Janie's screams pierced Vicki's heart.

TWELVE

Lenore's Struggle

VICKI opened the pantry door and jumped back as the locust skittered out, flapping wildly and screeching, "Apollyon! Apollyon!"

"I didn't know those things could talk," Conrad said. The locust flew past him and Conrad turned his head. "Disgusting."

Janie was still screaming, slapping at her legs and hair. "Get it off me! Get it off!"

"It's gone," Vicki said.

Janie quivered and twitched from her locust bite. The demonic venom was shooting through her veins. Vicki saw only one bite, on Janie's face, and it was beginning to swell. "Am I—am I going to die?" Janie managed.

"No," Vicki said. *But you'll wish you could,* Vicki thought.

Vicki and Conrad helped Janie into an upstairs room and tried to make her as comfortable as possible. When they returned downstairs, a dozen locusts were gathered around the door to the basement, biting, clawing, and scratching to get inside. One flew menacingly at Vicki and landed on her back. The thing hissed, as if trying to keep Vicki from helping the people downstairs.

Conrad knocked the locust off. "Plug any holes you can find. I'll see if I can get rid of these guys."

Conrad picked up a piece of firewood and swung at a hovering locust. He hit it solidly, and the creature crashed into the wall behind Vicki and fell to the floor.

Vicki bent over to inspect it. She was sickened by the sight but at the same time intrigued. "Conrad, come look at this."

The blow from the firewood had stunned the locust. Its segmented belly rose and fell as it breathed. Its body was shaped like a tiny horse armed for war. The thing had wings like a flying grasshopper.

"Fascinating," Conrad said as he inched closer. "It's a mix between a horse and a man."

"Look at those teeth," Vicki said.

The locust opened its eyes and screamed, "Apollyon!" It flew toward Vicki, but Conrad had a bead on it. He swung the wood and knocked the locust against the wall with a terrible blow. Vicki thought the beast would surely have cracked in two, but it lay in one piece, its wings clicking.

Conrad picked it up. "No wonder we can't kill the thing—its back feels stronger than the safe. And it's got little spines."

"Put it down," Vicki said.

"Grab that bucket by the fireplace," Conrad said. "We'll trap it."

Vicki brought the heavy bucket and put it upside down. Conrad held the locust close to her. "This is the stinger here. You can almost see through it. And that has to be the venom." A liquid substance sloshed as Conrad moved. "What do you think it's saying?"

"Tsion told us that the king over these things is the chief demon in the pit. He rules over all the demons of hell. In Greek the name is Apollyon. It's something different in Hebrew."

"If these really are demons," Conrad said, "they've got to want to kill us."

"But they can't," Vicki said. "Just shows you God can use even his enemy for his own purposes."

The creature opened its eyes. Vicki screamed. Conrad threw it on the floor and quickly put the bucket over it. The locust beat its wings against the bucket but couldn't get out. Inside, the tiny voice screamed again and again, "Apollyon! Apollyon!"

Mark ran back to the car and found Carl in the backseat, stuffing tissues and trash into a crack in one of the back windows. The locusts had found the spot and were trying to crawl through.

Mark found an empty beer bottle nearby and swatted the locusts away. The metal backs of the monsters pinged as Mark swung the glass.

"What are these things?" Carl yelled frantically.

"Demons," Mark said.

"Why aren't they bothering you?"

"They know I have the seal of God on my forehead," Mark said. "They can't hurt me."

Carl looked puzzled. "That stuff John told me about God . . . it's really true?"

Mark leaned close to the window. "It's your only hope against these things and against being separated from God forever."

"I came up here to tell you John's story," Carl yelled. "What he did haunts me. I read some of the stuff about God, but I felt so

worthless. I could never do what John did. I
don't deserve—"

"None of us deserves what God gives us,"
Mark said. "But he wants to forgive us and
make us part of his family."

"I want that," Carl said.

Another swarm of locusts descended on
the car. Their beating wings were deafening.
Some landed on Mark, hissing. He was
surprised by how much they weighed. He
shook them off and tried to clear the window. It was as if the demons didn't want
Mark to talk with Carl about God.

"What do I need to do?" Carl shouted.

"Pray with me," Mark said. "God, I'm sorry
for the bad things I've done. I believe Jesus
died for me and took my punishment.
Change me right now and make me your
child. And help me to live for you. In Jesus'
name, amen."

The locusts hissed as Carl said, "Amen."

Judd sat still as the plane taxied to the terminal. The locusts covered the plane, hissing
and chanting something. It sounded like, "A
bad one! A bad one!" Finally Judd recognized the word from having read Tsion
Ben-Judah's Web site. It was *Abbadon*, the

Hebrew word for the chief demon of the bottomless pit. "Abbadon, Abbadon," the locusts hissed, calling out to their demonic leader.

People around Judd were terrified, holding hands over their ears and crying. Judd knew if they did manage to get to the terminal, it was unlikely anyone would be able to help them connect the ramp. Already he could see baggage handlers and maintenance workers writhing in pain on the runway.

As they approached the terminal, Judd stood and squeezed into the aisle. He searched for anyone with the mark of the believer.

When he reached first class, a flight attendant yelled at him to sit down. He shook his head.

"Get back in your seat, sir, or I'll have to call the captain!" the flight attendant said.

"I want to volunteer," Judd said. "Those things out there are stinging people, but I can help."

The flight attendant pulled Judd into the galley and closed the curtain. She whispered, "I won't have you upsetting the passengers."

"I'm telling the truth," Judd said. "If those things get inside the plane, they'll sting everybody."

"Everybody but you?" the attendant said skeptically.

"I'm not a target. I can't explain right now why—"

"Then get to your seat. We're responsible for your safety and if you can't explain—"

"Okay," Judd said. "Since I believe in Jesus, those locusts won't bother me. They're only after people who . . . who don't believe in God."

"You're one of those people," the woman said. "I believe in God, but I don't follow that crazy rabbi."

The plane stopped. Judd put a hand out to steady himself. "You've got to believe me."

Passengers whimpered and cried. They were too frightened to retrieve their things from the overhead bins.

"Wait here," the attendant said.

A few moments later she returned with a member of the flight crew. "Linda said you've volunteered to go outside and help with the ramp," the pilot said. "All of our personnel are down."

Judd nodded. "If you can get me out of here without letting any of those things in, I can help. But if even one of them gets inside the cabin, it'll sting all the passengers."

Lionel felt sorry for the worker trapped outside the door, but he knew he couldn't risk opening it and letting the locusts inside. Besides, Lionel knew that once the man was stung, there was nothing anyone could do.

Lionel ran to a security worker. "You've got to seal off the terminal!"

The man seemed dazed. He nodded, then lifted his radio. "Seal off all the entrances to the terminal!"

Lionel found Sam, and they watched Judd's plane taxi toward the terminal. The smoky cloud that had hung over them for days was gone, but the spread of the demon locusts was as thick as the cloud had been. The locusts flew into the window, piling on top of each other to get a look inside.

A worker on the tarmac screamed and beat his head against the concrete. Lionel shook his head.

"He's going to kill himself," Sam said.

Lionel stared through the thousands of demons looking straight at them. "'In those days people will seek death but will not find it,'" he said, quoting the verse from memory. "'They will long to die, but death will flee away!'"

Mark peered through the car window, knocking away the locusts that kept coming. The car was covered with the beasts now, and he couldn't see Carl.

Mark raced to the other side and opened the door.

"Are you crazy?" Carl said.

Mark smiled. "Get out."

Carl's eyes darted from Mark's face to the locusts buzzing around his head. Carl slid out of the car. "They're not stinging me."

"They won't," Mark said, pointing to his forehead. "See this?"

"It's a cross," Carl said. "I didn't notice that when I first met you."

"You have one just like it. Come on," Mark said, "I want to get you back to meet the others. And I want to hear John's story."

Vicki checked on Janie later in the day. The girl thrashed and moaned. She shivered as if it were the middle of winter.

Conrad brought some cool cloths and stood by Vicki. "We gave her every chance."

Vicki nodded. Finally, Janie relaxed enough to speak. "Why didn't you tell me?"

"We tried," Vicki said. "You wouldn't listen."

"Why would God do such a thing to me?" Janie said. "I can't stand the pain."

"Give your life to God now, Janie," Vicki said.

"Will it make it stop hurting?" Janie said.

"I don't think so, but—"

"Then what good is your God anyway?" Janie yelled. "Get out! Both of you, get out!"

Conrad followed Vicki downstairs. They had closed every opening in the house and still the locusts were finding their way inside.

Vicki had prepared enough food and water downstairs to keep people alive for a few weeks. At some point they would need to get more supplies, assuming the locusts continued their attack. Vicki couldn't wait to log onto the Web and see what more Tsion Ben-Judah had to say.

Someone screamed downstairs. Darrion and Shelly were calling for help.

"Can you clear these bugs off the stairway door?" Vicki said.

"I'll do my best," Conrad said. He grabbed the piece of firewood and started whacking. There were at least a hundred locusts chewing, biting, and scratching to get inside. A few minutes later the locusts lay in a heap, stunned.

Vicki grabbed a flashlight from the kitchen and opened the stairwell door. She ducked inside and slammed it behind her, inspecting the basement as she walked downstairs. Locusts scratched on the walls, but none were inside.

She raced down the stairs to the secret entrance to the room below. She lifted the trapdoor and gasped. Charlie, Melinda, and Lenore cowered in one corner of the room. Shelly and Darrion stood by the tunnel door, their feet planted firmly in the dirt.

"They're digging through the mud underneath the door," Darrion shouted. "We can't hold them much longer!"

Vicki raced back to the room above and grabbed a loose board. Shelly screamed again. "One of them's getting through!"

"Come up here!" Vicki shouted, motioning for Charlie, Melinda, and Lenore to follow her.

The three scrambled up the stairs into the room. Shelly and Darrion struggled to keep the locusts from working through the mud. One of the demons clawed its way through and showed its ugly head. Shelly was terrified. She jumped back from the doorway just as Vicki brought the board and slapped it on the ground.

But it was too late. One of the demons flew into the room, its teeth bared, looking for a victim.

Lenore screamed from above, "My baby! Don't let it hurt my baby!"

Vicki glanced in the corner at the make-shift crib Charlie had made. Tolan was awake and thrashing under the covers.

The locust glanced at Vicki, Shelly, and Darrion, then darted for the corner. It hovered over the crib, its teeth dripping with venom.

"No!" Vicki shouted.

ABOUT THE AUTHORS

Jerry B. Jenkins (www.jerryjenkins.com) is the writer of the Left Behind series. He is author of more than one hundred books, of which eleven have reached the *New York Times* best-seller list. Former vice president for publishing for the Moody Bible Institute of Chicago, he also served many years as editor of *Moody* magazine and is now Moody's writer-at-large.

His writing has appeared in publications as varied as *Reader's Digest, Parade,* in-flight magazines, and many Christian periodicals. He has written books in four genres: biography, marriage and family, fiction for children, and fiction for adults.

Jenkins's biographies include books with Hank Aaron, Bill Gaither, Luis Palau, Walter Payton, Orel Hershiser, Nolan Ryan, Brett Butler, and Billy Graham, among many others.

Eight of his apocalyptic novels—*Left Behind, Tribulation Force, Nicolae, Soul Harvest, Apollyon, Assassins, The Indwelling,* and *The Mark*—have appeared on the Christian Booksellers Association's best-selling fiction list and the *Publishers Weekly* religion best-seller list. *Left Behind* was nominated for Book of the Year by the Evangelical Christian Publishers Association in 1997, 1998, 1999, and 2000. *The Indwelling* was number one on the *New York Times* best-seller list for four consecutive weeks.

As a marriage and family author and speaker, Jenkins has been a frequent guest on Dr. James Dobson's *Focus on the Family* radio program.

Jerry is also the writer of the nationally syndicated sports story comic strip *Gil Thorp,* distributed to newspapers across the United States by Tribune Media Services.

Jerry and his wife, Dianna, live in Colorado.

Dr. Tim LaHaye (www.timlahaye.com), who conceived the idea of fictionalizing an account of the Rapture and the Tribulation, is a noted author, minister, and nationally recognized speaker on Bible prophecy. He is the founder of both Tim LaHaye Ministries and The Pre-Trib Research Center. Presently Dr. LaHaye speaks at many of the major Bible prophecy conferences in the U.S. and Canada, where his nine current prophecy books are very popular.

Dr. LaHaye holds a doctor of ministry degree from Western Theological Seminary and the doctor of literature degree from Liberty University. For twenty-five years he pastored one of the nation's outstanding churches in San Diego, which grew to three locations. It was during that time that he founded two accredited Christian high schools, a Christian school system of ten schools, and Christian Heritage College.

Dr. LaHaye has written over forty books, with over 30 million copies in print in thirty-three languages. He has written books on a wide variety of subjects, such as family life, temperaments, and Bible prophecy. His current fiction works, written with Jerry Jenkins—*Left Behind, Tribulation Force, Nicolae, Soul Harvest, Apollyon, Assassins, The Indwelling,* and *The Mark*—have all reached number one on the Christian best-seller charts. Other works by Dr. LaHaye are *Spirit-Controlled Temperament; How to Be Happy Though Married; Revelation Unveiled; Understanding the Last Days; Rapture under Attack; Are We Living in the End Times?;* and the youth fiction series Left Behind: The Kids.

He is the father of four grown children and grandfather of nine. Snow skiing, waterskiing, motorcycling, golfing, vacationing with family, and jogging are among his leisure activities.

The Future Is Clear

Check out the exciting Left Behind: The Kids series

BOOKS #21 AND #22 COMING SOON!

Discover the latest about the Left Behind series and complete line of products at

www.leftbehind.com